### *When he'd touched her, it hadn't mattered who she was,*

who her father was, or what hold she had over everyone in this place. All that mattered was silky skin, heat, enormous blue eyes and the fragrance that clung to her that made him think of sunlight even in this storm.

When another flash of lightning ripped through the skies, bathing her in a white light that only succeeded in defining everything right about her, he muttered, "Impulses can be dangerous things." And he deliberately pushed his hands behind his back to kill his own impulses, then looked out at the storm that was building in force again.

"You don't even know me," she said softly.

He looked back at her, unsettled by how vulnerable she looked in that moment. "I know you shouldn't be here."

Dear Reader,

The year is winding to a close, with bare tree branches reaching for a cold gray sky, and chill winds howling around corners and through alleys. It's a bleak season, a perfect season for curling up under a thick blanket—and in front of a warm fire, if you have one—and seeing the old year out with the newest offerings from Silhouette Shadows.

This month we bring you two more of the eerie, goose-bump-inducing tales you've come to expect from the line: *False Family* by Mary Anne Wilson and *Shaded Leaves of Destiny* by new author Sally Carleen. As always, our talented writers have combined irresistible romance with spine-tingling spookiness, just for you.

And next year we'll be back, with more chills, more thrills, more darkly sensuous loving, right here in the shadows—Silhouette Shadows.

Enjoy!

Leslie Wainger
Senior Editor and Editorial Coordinator

Please address questions and book requests to:
Silhouette Reader Service
U.S.: 3010 Walden Ave., P.O. Box 1325, Buffalo, NY 14269
Canadian: P.O. Box 609, Fort Erie, Ont. L2A 5X3

# MARY ANNE WILSON

# False Family

Published by Silhouette Books
America's Publisher of Contemporary Romance

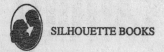 SILHOUETTE BOOKS

ISBN 0-373-27045-3

FALSE FAMILY

**Books by Mary Anne Wilson**

Silhouette Intimate Moments

*Hot-Blooded* #230
*Home Fires* #267
*Liar's Moon* #292
*Straight from the Heart* #304
*Dream Chasers* #336
*Brady's Law* #350
*Child of Mine* #374
*Nowhere To Run* #410
*Echoes of Roses* #438
*Two for the Road* #472
*Two Against the World* #489
*Jake's Touch* #574

Silhouette Shadows

*False Family* #45

*Sister, Sister

---

## MARY ANNE WILSON

fell in love with reading at ten years of age when she discovered *Pride and Prejudice*. A year later she knew she had to be a writer when she found herself writing a new ending for *A Tale of Two Cities*. A true romantic, she had Sydney Carton rescued, and he lived happily ever after.

Though she's a native of Canada, she now lives in California with her husband and a six-toed black cat who believes he's Hungarian and five timid Dobermans who welcome any and all strangers. And she's writing happy endings for her own books.

# PROLOGUE

*December 21*

The thunderstorm that tore through the San Francisco night was the perfect backdrop for murder.

Cold and violent, it blurred the flashing Christmas lights that adorned the businesses and homes in its torrential path, and it made the steep street outside the old Jenning's Theater slick and dangerous.

Few people ventured out into the pouring rain. A single person, the Watcher, came up the street, staying close to the chipped brick and wooden walls of the closed businesses. An umbrella barely blocked the sting of the torrent.

The Watcher slipped into the doorway of a store sharing a wall with the theater and observed the street in both directions. Few cars drove by, and the ticket booth under the marquee that announced *A Christmas Carol By Charles Dickens, December 10-30* was still shut.

As a bolt of lightning tore through the heavens, the flash of raw light exposed a woman in a dark raincoat, carrying a bright yellow umbrella as she hurried down the hill toward the theater. Once under the partial shelter of the theater portico, the woman slowed her pace and looked up.

Mallory King.

A riot of dark curls framed a delicate, heart-shaped face flushed from the effort of hurrying. With just a glance at the ticket booth, she veered to the left and into a side alley that led to the stage door. As she disappeared from sight, the Watcher sank back into the shadows.

She'd been easy enough to find. A bit-part actress who worked as a waitress in a restaurant three blocks down from the theater. A nothing person in the larger scheme, yet a person who could make another do desperate things. Killing someone was certainly desperate, but the only thing to do under the circumstances.

When Mallory King left the theater around eleven, she would head for the restaurant where she would work until 7:00 a.m. It was unsafe for any woman to walk on the streets of San Francisco, day or night. So it wouldn't be surprising if Mallory King never made it to the restaurant tonight, if she became another accident statistic....

# CHAPTER ONE

Magic and illusion ended when the lights came up and the curtains went down on a play. And the final curtain was coming down tonight for this play. It had been canceled with five days left on its run.

Poor box office and bad weather had combined to cut it short, and as Mallory King sat applying red lipstick in front of the makeup table in the long, narrow dressing room, she was mentally making a list of places she could go tomorrow to look for another job.

The door opened and a stagehand yelled, "One minute."

Mallory quickly finished applying the lipstick, then sat back and looked at herself in the mottled mirrors. Her ebony hair had been gathered on top of her head in a riot of curls contained by a holly wreath, and her sapphire blue eyes had been highlighted by dark mascara. Deep blush brought out her high cheek line, and the gauzy, full-length white dress she wore was off the shoulder and nipped in tightly at her waist with a white satin band.

"The Ghost of Christmas Past," she muttered at her reflection. That's just what this job had become—a ghost—and she didn't know what she would do if she didn't get something else quickly. She couldn't survive on what she made in tips at the restaurant.

She blotted her lips and stood as the door opened again. "You're on," the stagehand yelled into the room.

"I'm coming," she called back as she tossed a tissue into the wastebasket. Turning, she hurried to the door and stepped into the hallway, turning left toward backstage. But as she rounded the corner near the stage door, she ran right into an immovable object, and felt hands clamp on her shoulders to keep her from stumbling backward. As she looked up, fully expecting to see one of the stagehands, she was shocked to find it was a man she'd never seen before.

He was tall, at least three inches over six feet, and he wore a dark, well-cut trench coat. His rain-dampened raven black hair was slicked back from a face that was far from traditionally handsome, but with a sensuality that struck her instantly, with a force that shook her. His features seemed to be all harsh planes and angles, his skin deeply tanned, his nose strong and his jaw clean-shaven.

But it was his eyes that riveted Mallory, making her next breath almost impossible. They were slightly slanted, as black as the night outside, with short, spiked lashes, and they were staring at her with an unsettling intensity.

It took her a moment to realize that he exuded an aura of danger, which defied reason since he'd kept her from falling. But it was there and almost tangible. She had to try twice before she forced words past the tightness in her throat. "I'm sorry. I wasn't looking where I was going."

"No damage done," the man murmured in a low, rough voice as his hands released their hold on her. His dark eyes flicked over her in a heartbeat. "You look like a ghost."

She nervously smoothed the fine, white material of her dress. "The Ghost of Christmas Past."

He inclined his head slightly as his eyes narrowed. "My guess would have been the Ghost of Christmas Present," he muttered, his expression tightening as he spoke.

This wasn't any light banter, impersonal conversation between strangers. There was an edge to it that disturbed Mallory, almost as much as the man inches from her. Right then she heard the beginning strains of the musical piece that signaled her entrance, and the stranger was blocking her path to stage left. "For tonight, it's Christmas Past," she said. "That's my cue. I need to—"

"Break a leg," he murmured, then stood aside to let her pass.

Mallory ducked her head and hurried by him to her spot. The music swelled, and as the stagehand pulled the curtain back for her to step onto the stage, she could feel eyes on her. The stranger was watching her.

With a quick look back as she stepped forward, she saw the man had moved into the shadows near the prop room. But that didn't diminish the intensity of his gaze on her. She'd never reacted like this to a man, attracted to him, yet aware of a danger that surrounded him. It had seemed like forever since she even looked at a man with anything more than passing interest.

When he nodded to her, she looked away. Then, as the actor playing Scrooge called, "Who goes there?" she took a shaky breath and stepped through the curtains into the light. In the next instant she was part of the fantasy she created on stage, a fantasy that didn't have a place for a dark stranger who disturbed her and made her feel vulnerable.

At one minute to ten, the fantasy ended, and reality came back with a thud. Mallory had made her way back to the dressing room, which was crowded with the other female members of the cast. She had looked back over her shoulder more than once in the hallway, half expecting to see the stranger lingering in the shadows.

But he was nowhere in sight. And once inside, she stripped off her costume, put on her old terry-cloth robe and sat down in front of the mirrors. Methodically she began to spread cold cream on her face, and as she removed the last of the heavy stage makeup, lightning ripped through the night outside, its white glow flashing into the room through the bank of high windows, which were filmed with the grime of the city.

She tossed the last makeup-soiled cotton ball in the trash, then looked at her reflection in the mottled mirrors. She looked tired, her face pale in contrast to her dark hair, as she released her curls from the holly wreath. Her eyes were smudged with shadows from the sleeplessness she'd experienced over the past few days.

She grimaced, her natural ability to ignore the reality of the present and fantasize about a better future almost failing her right then. That little part of her life where she could make-believe and become someone else, that part that took her away from her job as a waitress and the empty apartment where she lived, had been taken from her until she could find another part in another play.

As she tossed the holly wreath into the prop box, she heard someone yell over the din, "King! Mallory King!"

She twisted to look back to the door and saw a stagehand waving in her direction. When he made eye contact with her, he called, "You've got a visitor!"

Mallory was surprised. She had never had anyone come backstage to see her after a play, and the house had been less than half-full during the performance. The applause at the curtain call had been more from politeness than enthusiasm. Then she remembered the man she'd run into, and for a second she thought he might have come back. But why would he?

She pointed to herself. "Me?"

The stagehand nodded, then ducked out and shut the door.

She stood and tugged her robe around her, knotting the tie at her waist as she made her way through the room. Nearing the door, she put the idea of the stranger out of her mind. It was crazy. When she opened the door and stepped into the dimly lit hallway, she spotted someone by the outside doors.

It was a woman. She recognized Elaine Bowers, her agent. Elaine, with her short, gray-blond hair curling slightly from the humidity. She was wearing a dark raincoat over a simple gray suit. "Mallory," she said as she crossed to her.

Mallory slowly closed the door and watched the woman approach. One glance around the hallway and she knew that the dark-haired stranger wasn't lingering in any of the nooks and crannies in the dingy space. She focused on the woman in front of her. Mallory knew she was one of her agent's least lucrative clients, and she certainly didn't warrant a personal visit on such a rainy night. "Elaine, what are you doing here?" Mallory asked.

The short, plump woman looked at her watch. "Looking for you." She glanced up and down the hallway, grimacing at the faded walls and the low, moisture-stained ceiling. "Boy, I haven't been in here in years. This old place was once *the* theater in the city. Can you believe it?"

"If you go out into the foyer and narrow your eyes, you can almost see how it must have looked years ago."

"My imagination isn't that good."

"Right now, mine isn't too good, either. I've been trying to imagine why you're here, and I can't come up with anything."

"I was contacted by a Mr. Welting, an attorney who I'm supposed to meet here." She took one last look over her shoulder, then moved a bit closer to Mallory. "I wanted to get here a few minutes before him so I could explain a bit to you before he showed up."

Mallory tugged her robe more tightly around her. "Explain what to me?"

"This whole business is so rushed and odd," she muttered with a shake of her head. "Mr. Welting contacted me just before five this afternoon. He's an attorney for Saxon Mills."

"Saxon Mills? Money, business, wine," Mallory muttered. "What was his attorney doing contacting you?"

"Offering you a job."

Mallory almost laughed. "A job for me? Well, I'm desperate, so if he wants me to crush grapes, tell him I'm willing."

Elaine flicked that away with one hand and only the shadow of a smile. "No, he wants you for an acting job."

"That's even better. I'll take it."

"You don't even know what *it* is."

"They're closing the play as of tonight, Elaine. I'm free *and* broke. I'll take anything."

"I thought they might have to close. With this lousy weather and the economy, it's hard to keep small companies going."

"And the restaurant's cutting back, too. I've lost two of my shifts, so I need whatever I can get."

"Then this'll work out better than I thought. It's good timing for everyone."

"It is for me. Now, what's the part and when do I start?"

"Tomorrow, actually, and it runs through New Year's. You're going in as a replacement for someone. One of Welting's people saw you when you were working at the Garnet last month in the Simon play. He remembered you when this position came up, and

Mr. Welting says that you're just right for what they want."

"What play is it?"

Elaine looked a bit embarrassed. The woman usually had an answer for every question. "I'm sorry. This all happened so fast I didn't get that. But when the man gets here, you can get all the details. All I know is, it's in the Napa Valley area, a dinner theater of sorts, and they're doing a Christmas piece."

Sara Springer, the actress who played Tiny Tim's oldest sister, came out of the dressing room and met Mallory. "I'm going down the block to pick up some pizzas for everyone, sort of a holiday wake. Do you want some?"

"No thanks."

"Do you mind if I use your umbrella to go? Mine blew inside-out on the way here."

"No, go ahead."

"Thanks," Sara said before she went back into the dressing room.

Mallory turned back to Elaine. "It's up in Napa?"

"That's what he said."

"Then I don't see how I can do it. I've got the restaurant—what little time they're giving me—and commuting would be too much. My car's on its last legs, as it is, and that would kill it."

"Actually, you'll have to forget about the restaurant for a while and stay in Napa if you want this job."

"I can't afford to—"

"Listen, you're being offered a per diem and three times scale. Mr. Welting said it was an emergency.

They're willing to pay what they need to get you to take over the part."

Mallory did some fast figuring and realized that even though she didn't celebrate Christmas or put any stock in it, she was getting a genuine holiday present with this job. She could last at least two months on that money, even without working at the restaurant. "I guess I can't refuse. But I'll have to contact the restaurant and see what I can work out with them."

"Good." Elaine looked very relieved. "I knew you'd do it."

The stage door opened abruptly, and for a moment the storm invaded the narrow hallway with pouring rain and a cold wind that curled around Mallory's bare legs. Then a man ducked inside, a blur of dark clothes and height. The stranger. He'd come back, and for a second her heart lurched with the idea that he was the attorney Elaine had told her about.

But as he turned and brushed at his raincoat, then skimmed off a dark fedora he was wearing, she knew how wrong she'd been. He might be tall, but he was totally bald and more slight, with a pallor to his complexion that was in sharp contrast to the black coat. He could have been anywhere from fifty to seventy, with a narrow, furrowed face that looked devoid of any tendency to humor.

He spotted Elaine and headed right for her. "Ms. Bowers," he said in a clipped voice that was tinged by a nasal quality. "I am sorry for the slight delay."

"No problem, Mr. Welting," Elaine said as the man stopped in front of her. "It gave me a chance to fill Mallory in on what you need."

"Excellent," he murmured, turning to look at Mallory.

Pale blue eyes, under bushy gray brows, narrowed, as the man pointedly stared at her with no hint of apology. His gaze traveled over her in what would have been a suggestive way if there had been any sexual overtones to it. But there were none. His scrutiny was cold and calculating, and as emotion free as the stranger's gaze had earlier been emotion laden.

"You will do just fine," he finally murmured, then gave her an oddly formal partial bow. "I am Henry Welting, representing Mr. Saxon Mills. It is a pleasure meeting you, Ms. King."

She wished she could say the same, but the man made her skin crawl. "Elaine was just explaining your job offer to me."

"Did she outline the financial aspects of the offer?"

"We went through all of it," Elaine said quickly.

"And it's satisfactory?" he said, never looking away from Mallory.

"Yes, it's satisfactory," Mallory said.

"Good. I would hate to haggle over a few dollars."

The pay wasn't exactly a "few dollars" to Mallory, but to a man wearing obviously expensive, hand-tailored clothes, the money was probably a pittance. "She also mentioned a per diem."

"Yes, of course. Since it's not in this area, we thought it best to offer you that." He stared at her without blinking as he lifted one eyebrow slightly. "Since you are basically alone in the world, we didn't feel that there would be any problem with relocating for the two weeks. There won't be, will there?''

She was taken aback by his statement about her personal life, but said simply, ''No problem at all.''

''Then you accept the offer?''

She didn't like this man, but she didn't have to like him to do the job. ''Yes, I'll take the job.''

''Excellent,'' he said. ''Mr. Mills will be very pleased. The contracts will be at Ms. Bowers's office tomorrow morning at nine for signatures.'' He reached into the inside pocket of his trench coat with his free hand and took out an envelope that he offered to Mallory. ''These are instructions to be followed *to the letter.*''

She took the thin envelope and glanced at her name typed neatly on the front. ''And the script?'' she asked, looking back at Mr. Welting.

''That will all be given to you when you report for work.''

''But, I—''

He kept speaking as if she hadn't said a thing. ''It is very important that you follow the instructions exactly. You are to report to Mr. Mills at his home at precisely six o'clock tomorrow evening.''

''His home?''

''Mr. Mills is taking care of this personally, and he seldom leaves his home anymore. When you meet with him, he will explain everything to you.''

''Is there anything else?''

He slipped his hat back on. ''You are to discuss this with no one until you see Mr. Mills. Anything else you might need to know is in the envelope.'' He stared at her for a long, awkward moment before he said, "What is it they say in the theater for good luck, Ms. King? Break a leg?"

It took Mallory aback to hear that phrase for the second time in the last few hours. "Thanks," she murmured at the same time Sara came back out of the dressing room with another actress. Both were dressed in dark raincoats, and Sara was carrying Mallory's umbrella. As she headed down the hallway, Sara accidentally bumped Mr. Welting on his arm.

The man jerked back and glared at her. "Sorry," Sara muttered. Then with a "We'll be right back" to Mallory, she and the other girl headed for the stage entrance.

As the two of them stepped out into the storm and the door shut behind them, Mr. Welting said, "I think that's all that's needed here. My driver is waiting for me." He inclined his head to Mallory. "Thank you for agreeing to help Mr. Mills. I know he will be very appreciative of it." He glanced at Elaine. "Thank you for taking care of this so expeditiously, Ms. Bowers."

"Of course," she murmured.

With a fleeting look back at Mallory, he turned and headed for the doors. Without glancing back, he pushed back the metal barrier and stepped out into the night. Then he was gone and the door closed with a creaking moan.

Mallory exhaled and leaned back against the wall as she stared at the door. "Boy, he's strange. It's a night for meeting strange people."

"Forget about him. You don't have to deal with him anymore. I'll take care of any other business things that come up."

Mallory looked back at Elaine. "It all seems so odd, doesn't it?"

"Listen, I can understand if you're a bit uneasy about this, but I can assure you, I checked this all out. Henry Welting does a number of things for Saxon Mills, both professionally and personally. He's been on retainer for the man for over fifteen years. The offer's very legitimate. I wouldn't let you do it if I thought there was anything shady about it."

"Sure, of course," Mallory murmured, then looked back at the door as it flew open, and the girl who had left with Sara rushed back into the hallway. Her face was as white as a sheet, and rain dripped from her hair and her drenched clothes.

"Call an ambulance!" she gasped.

Mallory stood straight. "What's wrong?"

"It's Sara. She—" The girl was beginning to shake all over. "She . . . she was in front of me, crossing the street, and a car . . . it hit her." She swiped at her face with a trembling hand. "I think she's dead."

*December 22*

The fury of the storm let up for little more than half a day before it came back again in earnest. At five the next afternoon, Mallory was driving north on an all-but-deserted two-lane road. Wind shook her small car, and rain beat relentlessly against the oxidized blue paint.

The rolling hills that formed the valley and were covered with vineyards on either side of the road were almost obliterated by the storm and the shadows of the coming night. Mallory sat forward, straining to make out the wooden road signs through the rain and the slapping of the windshield wipers.

The written directions she had been given were simple enough. They just hadn't mentioned how to cope with what seemed like a hurricane.

Mallory gripped the steering wheel so tightly that her fingers ached, and no matter how intently she tried to focus her thoughts, she couldn't forget the horror of last night. The moments after her friend's accident had been filled with total confusion—flashing lights, sirens and Sara laying on the asphalt, her arms and legs askew at unnatural angles, her blood from a massive head wound mingling with the rain on the pavement.

No one had seen the car until it ran Sara down, and no one knew what happened to it afterward. Hit-and-run. And it had left Sara alive...but just barely. When she'd been taken to the hospital, they'd found compound fractures of her forearm and thigh. By far the most serious injury had been the head wound. She'd undergone emergency surgery in the small hours of the morning to relieve pressure on her brain and the doctors were guardedly optimistic.

Mallory had stayed until morning, when Sara's parents arrived. They had been devastated, and when Mallory was leaving, they were sitting on either side of their unconscious daughter, holding her hands, talking softly to her, encouraging her to come back to them.

For one fleeting moment, Mallory had almost felt envious of poor Sara. Mallory had never known her father. He'd walked out on her mother before Mallory had been born. And the memories of her mother were vague, distorted remembrances of a five-year-old child. Dark hair, a soft voice, eyes touched with a sadness that never quite disappeared. Nothing substantial.

And Mallory knew if she was in the bed instead of Sara, no one would be crying for her. She had no one. Henry Welting had said she was "basically alone," but the reality was, she was completely alone. Just as alone as she was on this road right now. She couldn't see any lights, and only a handful of cars had passed her since she left Napa.

Her headlights cut into the darkness and rain, and she caught a glimpse of a sign ahead. As she slowed, she could barely make out dark lettering on an old-fashioned wooden road sign—Reece Place. With a sigh of relief, she made the left turn onto an even-narrower road that angled upward. A canopy of ancient trees on either side bent under the force of the wind and rain.

The road curved to the left and Mallory shifted to a lower gear to negotiate it, but even so, she felt the tires on the car spin for a second before they caught traction again. Yet before she could get the car fully under control, the road cut sharply to the right and as the car went into the curve, Mallory knew she wasn't going to make it.

In that split second, the car began to drift sideways on the slick pavement. Mallory felt the loss of control, the futility of pressing on the brakes and turning the wheel. She felt the stunning terror of knowing she could die. She felt sadness for what might have been, a sadness she had never let herself feel before.

Then the impact came. The car hit something solid, stopping with a bone-jarring suddenness, and the seat belt bit into her shoulder as Mallory felt her head jerk sideways.

Then it was all over. With the engine dead, the car tilted to the right, sinking slowly into the soft shoulder of the road. Finally it settled, and Mallory was thankful to be alive. The windshield wipers kept trying to clear the glass of the sheeting rain. The headlights were at a skewed angle, shooting up into the night, and the strength of the storm made the car shudder.

She slowly released her grip on the steering wheel, fumbled with the safety belt, then sank back into the seat. Looking to her right, she could make out the dark smear of grass and leaves pressed against the window. *She* might have survived, but the car wasn't going anywhere. She glanced at the dash clock. She had twenty minutes to get to Saxon Mills's house. There was no way she could make it.

"Merry Christmas to me," she muttered, feeling as if this gift of a job had been snatched right out of her grasp.

She closed her eyes, trying to figure out what to do. She didn't have any idea how far she'd have to walk through the storm to get to Mills Way. But if she sat here and waited for help, there was no guarantee anyone would come along tonight.

She looked out at the night and faced her options. She could feel the wind pushing at the car, and the rain seemed to be even heavier now. She turned off the headlights, then switched the key to the accessory position and flipped on the radio.

The strains of country music filled the confines of the small car, and for a while Mallory waited. But when the weather forecast came on, she reached to turn up the volume.

"And now for the Bay Area forecast. After a long drought that has forced water rationing for the past two years, the city is being deluged by a storm coming from the north, bringing torrential rain, winds gusting to forty miles an hour and temperatures in the midforties. Flooding has been reported in the low areas of the city, and mud slides have closed several roads leading into the valleys to the east and into Mill Valley to the north. With only scattered gaps in the weather front, the forecast is for a cold and very wet holiday season."

Mallory reached for the radio button and turned it off. A miserable twenty-four hours was getting worse by the minute. Sara's accident, the restaurant giving her no guarantee she could get her old job when she got back in two weeks, and now the job with Saxon Mills, which was dissolving right before her eyes.

She glanced at the dash clock. She had fifteen minutes to get to the meeting. Fifteen minutes. She sat forward and snapped on the headlights again. She could barely make out the fact that she was half on and half off the road. That road lead to Mills Way, and Mills Way led to Saxon Mills's house. In the next second, she made up her mind.

She wasn't going to let the Mills job go that easily. She had a raincoat, an umbrella and shoes that wouldn't be any worse if they got wet. No, the umbrella was gone. She could remember it lying on the road near Sara, torn and flattened. She pushed that thought out of her mind.

She had a hood on her raincoat, and it didn't matter what she looked like for the interview. Saxon Mills would just have to understand. As long as she made it. She turned the key, leaving it in the ignition, then tugged her hood up over her hair. Hesitating for only a moment as wind again shook the car, she faced the fact that walking was her only chance of salvaging anything with Saxon Mills.

She took her wallet out of her purse, shoved the purse under the front seat and tucked the wallet in her coat pocket. Then she pushed the door open against the wind and scrambled out. Her feet struck the edge of the pavement, and she levered herself up, ignoring the rain stinging her face until she was on her feet. Then the force of the wind snatched the door out of her grasp and slammed it with a resounding crack.

As Mallory turned, her feet slipped on the slick ground and she grabbed at the car to steady herself. She turned her back against the wind to look up the road ahead of her, then started off. But she hadn't taken more than two steps on the asphalt when she heard the roar of an engine behind her.

Filled with relief that someone had come, she spun around, and the hood of her coat was wrenched off her hair by the wind. As the headlights blinded her, and the squeal of brakes filled the air along with the scent of burning rubber, the relief was changed to fear in a single heartbeat. The car was coming right at her.

# CHAPTER TWO

$E$verything happened so quickly. There were blinding lights, the squeal of brakes and horror surging within her. As if the world had been reduced to slow motion, Mallory saw the headlights dip down from the force of the brakes grabbing the pavement, then, miraculously, the car stopped, inches from the back of her car, not from her.

She heard the engine throbbing, and the smell of burned rubber was in the air. Relief swelled up inside her as she realized the driver hadn't been heading for *her*. The things that had happened in the last twenty-four hours had left her nerves raw.

Mallory gulped air into her tight lungs and rubbed her trembling hands on her raincoat, almost giddy from relief. As she fumbled with her hood, trying to tug it back over her now-soaked hair, she heard a car door slam and saw movement. A hulking shadow emerged from the idling car, then came toward her.

The driver cut in front of the headlights, and Mallory could make out a tall man in a dark coat, carrying an umbrella. He strode directly for her. Nerves that were painfully jittery tingled as she was struck by how vulnerable she was on a dark, deserted road, at night, alone, with no protection at all.

By the time the idea of getting back in her car and locking the door had formed, the man was right in front of her. She pushed her hands into her pockets and curled them into tight fists to stop their trembling, while she carefully watched the stranger silhouetted in the headlights.

"What in the hell's going on?" The voice that came out of the stormy night was rough, deep and angry. "I didn't see you until I was almost on you!"

"I missed the curve, and the car... it went out of control. That's where it ended up."

"Did you hit something?" he asked, his body partially blocking the lights. The darkness seemed to surround the man, and the driving rain blurred everything.

"I lost control, and the car fishtailed. It sank in the mud on the shoulder." She found herself talking quickly, as nervousness grew in her. "It's stuck, and I thought I might just as well walk for help than sit here in the storm. I didn't think anyone would be coming this way."

"Where did you think you were walking to on this road?"

"I was looking for Mills Way."

He took a step closer to her, and she had to fight the urge to match that step backward to keep what buffer she could between them. "Mills Way?"

Cold rain found its way under her collar and trickled down her back, sending a chill through her. "Yes, I'm supposed to be meeting someone who lives on that road."

"Saxon Mills." It wasn't a question, just a statement.

"How did—?"

"There's only one house on that road." The man shifted, and the headlights shone directly on her once again. Although she couldn't see his eyes or even his expression, she knew he was staring at her…hard. She had a flashing memory of the man at the theater the night before and how thankful she'd been that she hadn't met him on a dark, deserted road.

The chill in her deepened. Her thoughts were going off on tangents that made no sense, and she narrowed her eyes against the glare. "I just want to get to that road."

"I could have killed you," he finally muttered.

Mallory felt her chest tighten, the memory of Sara lying on the rainy street so vivid that she ached. She'd been through too much, and her imagination was running wild in the most horrible way tonight. She pushed her hands deeper into her pockets and hunched her shoulders a bit as the rain beat down. "It's my fault. I never thought—"

"You should have put on your hazard lights. Anyone coming around that curve could plow right into your car."

"I didn't think about that, either." The temperature felt as if it had dropped ten degrees in the last few minutes. "I just need to get to Saxon Mills's home. Is there any way you could take me to a pay phone or to a house where I could call from?"

She didn't expect him to say, "I can take you all the way to Mills's estate."

As soon as he agreed, Mallory realized it hadn't been the smartest thing to say to a total stranger—offering to get into his car and drive off into the night. She tried to backtrack a bit. "It might be better if I stay with my car, and you can call a garage to come and pull me out of the mud."

"You can do that, but I'm afraid this isn't the city. There's no garage that would be open now. But if you want to wait here, I'll call when I get to a phone and maybe you'll get lucky. If not, lock the doors and someone will be here in the morning."

Mallory had taken care of herself since she was barely a teenager, and maybe she hadn't made the best decisions in the world, but she had often survived on her instinct. And right now her instinct for survival told her to take the ride, thank the man, get to Mills's house and try to salvage the job if she could. "I don't want to wait here all night," she admitted. "I'll take the ride."

"Then put on your emergency lights and let's get going."

Mallory didn't have to be told twice. She went to her car, opened the door, reached inside, pushed the button for the emergency lights, and they began to flash brilliant yellow into the rain and night. She closed the door, and as she turned, she stumbled on the slippery ground.

The man had her by the upper arm in the next second, his strong fingers pressing through the cotton of her soaked raincoat and steadying her. Mallory felt as if one of the bolts of lightning had shot through her at the contact, then he was urging her toward his car. "Let's get out of here," he said, close to her side.

By moving quickly ahead of him, she broke the contact. Keeping her head down to watch her footing on the rain-soaked road, she got to the car and could make out the dark shape of a low sports car with an engine that purred with a throaty idle. An expensive car.

Mallory circled to the passenger side, but before she could open the door, the man was there, reaching around her to pull the handle up. He was so close that Mallory felt his heat, and she inhaled the mingled scent of rain, mellow after-shave and a certain maleness. Then the door was open, and Mallory quickly got into the brown leather interior lit softly by dome and side lights.

She saw a dash that glowed with red-and-green gages, and instruments that would make a jet plane look simple. As the door closed, the interior lights went out. Mallory settled in the bucket seat and pushed the hood from her wet hair and swiped at the hair clinging to her face, then turned as the driver's door opened.

The interior lights flashed on again as the stranger easily maneuvered his rangy frame behind the leather-covered steering wheel. As he turned to push the umbrella into the area behind the front seats, Mallory got a clear look at him and she felt her breath catch.

The man from the theater, as dark as the night itself, and as disturbing as the storm that crashed around them outside. "You," she breathed.

He looked right at her as he ran a hand over his damp black hair, slicking it back from his roughly handsome face. "The Ghost of Christmas Past," he murmured, his dark eyes unblinking and intense in their scrutiny.

"How could...?" She touched her tongue to her lips. She could sense that aura of danger he had exuded last night at the theater, and that sensuality, as well, and she felt uncomfortable in these closed quarters. "How could you be here?"

The wind caught the door and slammed it shut, cutting off the lights inside, but it did nothing to diminish the impact of finding herself in this man's car. He turned to settle behind the wheel. "I drove and didn't go into a ditch."

"I'm not in a ditch," she said, hating the way her breathing tightened and her heartbeat refused to settle into a normal rhythm. She was totally alone with this man, and every nerve in her body was on edge.

"You're stuck," he pointed out as he put the car in gear, the windshield wipers swiping at the sheeting rain. The car moved to the left and headed up the road.

"What were you doing at the theater?" she asked.

"I like live theater."

She hadn't had any sense that he belonged at the theater when she'd run into him. "You're connected with the theater?"

"No, I got lost going to the men's room." He maneuvered a sharp corner, then headed uphill. "I hear the play closed, that what I saw was the last performance."

"Yes, it was." She stared at him as she nervously fingered the wet fabric of her coat. She could see little of him beyond a blurred profile touched by the low lights from the dash. "It just isn't a good time for small theater companies right now."

"Since it's already closed, I guess the bad publicity about the accident won't hurt it."

"Excuse me?"

"The hit-and-run victim outside the theater. I understood that she was a cast member."

The words were said evenly and without emotion, but they set Mallory's stomach into knots. "She was."

"She died?"

"No, she's still alive." Mallory closed her eyes for a moment, then exhaled and looked back at the man. "How did you know about all that?"

"The newspaper."

She hadn't even thought about the accident making the news. "The car never stopped. It's so senseless. If she hadn't gone out just then, or if it hadn't been raining..."

"Life boils down to chance, doesn't it?"

"A lot of times it does." She forced her hands to stop clenching and pressed them on the damp fabric of her coat by her thighs. "What are you doing out here in this storm?"

"Chance," he said softly. "The same as getting lost on the way to the rest room and meeting a ghost."

She nibbled on her lip as tension grew in her neck and shoulders. "That's no answer."

He ignored her statement and asked, "Is Saxon Mills expecting you?"

"Yes. I'm supposed to be there at six."

"You're going to be late."

She glanced at the digital clock in the dash, surprised to see that it was only five minutes to six. It seemed as if she had been on the road with this man for an eternity, but it had been less than ten minutes.

"If I get there close to six, I think it will be all right," she said, hoping it was true.

"Seeing him is pretty important to you, isn't it?"

"Yes it is, and I really appreciate you giving me a ride," she said, realizing she should have said those words a lot sooner. But surprise had robbed her of logical thinking for a few moments.

Right then, the man turned onto a narrow lane. As Mallory looked ahead of them, a cracking bolt of lightning lit the sky, exposing trees pressing on both sides and rain that ran down the pavement like a river. Then the light was gone, thunder pealed, and the only glow in the blackness came from the headlights of the sports car.

"You're going there for the holidays?"

"Not entirely."

"Business, too?"

Another bolt of lightning tore through the night, and thunder followed close on its heels. "It's getting closer," she said.

"Excuse me?"

"The lightning. When you see lightning, you start counting one thousand one, one thousand two. And whatever number you get up to before you hear the thunder, that's how many miles you are from the strike point of the lightning. That last lightning struck only a mile or so from here."

"Is that a scientific fact, or an old wives' tale?"

"I think it's scientific."

"Or maybe it was created to take people's attention off the storm."

She glanced at him again. "A diversion?"

"Yes, sort of like you're doing right now when I asked you that question."

"Excuse me?"

"I asked if you were seeing Saxon Mills on business and I was given the theory behind calculating the distance of lightning when it strikes."

"I'm going there to see Mr. Mills," she said. "That's it. Period."

"I was just trying to figure out what's so important that you were willing to go out on a night like this."

The more he prodded at her for details, the more she dug in her heels. She wasn't about to tell him exactly what she was doing on a road in this storm with his car hurtling toward her. "I didn't expect the storm to keep up so long." She laughed, a forced sound at best. "Besides, everyone knows we're in a drought situation in California. Now they're saying there's no end in sight to the storm."

"Who are you?" he asked abruptly.

"Mallory King. Who are you?" She deliberately said the question echoing his abruptly blunt tone.

"Anthony Carella. Where are you from?"

"The city." She felt annoyance at the man's curt tone of interrogation and repeated his words back to him. "Where are *you* from?"

"Los Angeles."

"Why were you at the theater in San Francisco?"

He was silent for a moment as he downshifted, slowing the car to a crawl. Then he glanced at her, his look lost in the shadows. He was silent for a long moment, then he turned back to the road ahead of them. "All right. I get the idea."

"What idea?"

"I tend to interrogate people. It's a bad habit of mine."

*And you never answered my question about the theater,* she thought, but didn't ask it again. "What are you—a lawyer?"

"No. Just a businessman."

She sat back in the seat. "Are you going somewhere for the holidays, or are you going somewhere on business?"

She could see him shrug, the movement sharp in the shadows. "Both. I'm going to see an associate of mine, and it happens to be the holidays." He cast her a fleeting glance as he slowed the car a bit more. "To answer your earlier question, I heard from a reliable source that I'd find the play interesting."

"You like Dickens?"

"I like interesting things," he murmured.

Mallory looked ahead of them and saw they were at the end of the road, facing a pair of massive stone pillars caught in the watery glow of the headlights. Imposing iron gates were open, and the car drove through onto a rough, cobbled drive that wound to the right. Wind shook the low car as it climbed upward. Then, as it crested the rise, two bolts of lightning ripped through the sky, one right on top of the other.

The eerie blue-white light exposed the scene in front of Mallory for no more than a split second, yet the images seemed to burn into her brain.

On a hill that rose out of a sea of rain-beaten grass dotted by trees that were almost bent to the ground by the wind, stood a looming structure that for all the world looked like a medieval castle. Corner turrets rose high into the turbulent night sky, and narrow windows glowed faintly gold from the interior lights. The drive wound up toward a jutting portico supported by huge pillars, and low lights lined sweeping steps that climbed to the entrance.

"This is Saxon Mills's home?" she breathed as thunder rumbled.

"You sound surprised."

She sat forward as they approached it, straining to make out more details, but unable to see little more now than the hulking shape and the dim glow of light at the windows and stairs. "I am, and I'm impressed. I've heard about the man being eccentric, but this looks like a castle."

"I think the resemblance to a castle is more than coincidental." As they neared the portico, the headlights swept in front of them, exposing rough stone walls that shimmered with rain. "If you know Saxon Mills at all, you know he gets some sort of a rush out of taking on the mantle. Actually, I don't believe he'd mind if you chose to worship him."

Mallory looked at the man. "Mr. Carella—"

"Tony," he said, correcting her. "I don't go along with formal royalty in this country."

"It sounds as if you don't like Saxon Mills very much."

He eased the car under the portico and stopped at the foot of the stairs, which led up to twenty-foot doors set in the heavy stone walls. The wind drove rain under the protection of the overhang, but the heaviest part of the downpour was blocked. "Whether I like him or not isn't important. I know what he is. That's the bottom line."

"He's an eccentric millionaire," she said.

"A billionaire, and he's much more than eccentric."

"Whatever," she murmured, glancing at the dash clock. "I'm already fifteen minutes late. Thanks for the ride. I really appreciate it." She turned to get out, but before she could touch the handle, Tony stopped her.

His fingers circled her wrist, cool and firm. The shock of his touch when he'd gripped her arm earlier was nothing compared to this. Skin-on-skin contact jolted her, and his fingers were tight, hovering just this side of inflicting pain. She sat very still and darted him a cautious look.

Even with the shimmering light of the house lamps coming through the rain-streaked windows, Tony was in the shadows, the glow not penetrating the darkness that seemed to surround him. When she tugged at the confines of his hold, she was freed, but she knew it was only because he allowed her to break the contact.

If this had been a match of strength, she knew she wouldn't stand a chance.

"What is it?" she asked, forcing herself not to rub at her wrist, which still tingled from the contact.

"Don't you want to know about Saxon Mills?"

Even though his eyes were hidden by shadows, Mallory could feel the intensity of his gaze on her. "You told me, he's an eccentric billionaire. What more is there to know?"

His hand gripped the top of the steering wheel so tightly that Mallory thought he would snap it. "That's a PR release, not the facts. The old man's known publicly for what he's made work in this world. But privately he's known for destroying anything that gets in his way or doesn't measure up to his standards. Everything and everyone is expendable for Saxon Mills. Everyone."

Intensity vibrated in his deep voice, and Mallory knew that to say this man didn't like Saxon Mills was akin to saying the Grand Canyon was a little hole in the ground. He obviously hated the old man. "Is that all?" she asked.

"Yes, it is."

She hesitated, then quickly turned from Tony and made her escape. Even under the protection of the portico, the wind drove the rain along the ground, and the stinging mists whipped around her legs. She hurried to the stone stairs, but as she reached the bottom step, she was shocked to sense Tony near her.

He didn't speak as he passed her and strode up the steps, taking them two at a time with his long stride. Mallory glanced back at the sports car to find its lights out and the motor off. She turned and hurried up after Tony, and when she caught up with him at the front doors, she looked up at him. His height was intimidating, and it made her feel at a distinct disadvantage.

"You don't have to see me in," she said as she tugged her coat more tightly around her.

"I know." He reached for a door knocker that was fashioned like a gargoyle head, the perfect touch to go with this house. With just a fleeting glance at Mallory in the glow of the lanterns by the doors, he released the knocker and the metal struck the barrier with a resounding crack. Even before the sound died out completely, the door clicked, then opened.

The glow of interior lights spilled out into the night and a woman looked out. She was tall, almost six feet, and dressed in a high-necked gray dress that wasn't quite a uniform, but was severely plain on her lanky frame. Her gray-streaked brown hair was pulled back from a long face touched by fine lines and decided paleness. Sensible wire-rimmed glasses reflected back the low lights and effectively hid her eyes, but Mallory didn't miss the way the woman's lips thinned as she looked at her.

"Good evening," she said with a nod to Mallory.

"Myra," Tony said.

"Mr. Carella." She inclined her head slightly, and the light shifted so Mallory got a glimpse of the woman's eyes. Gray eyes, the color of fog, were framed by pale lashes and looked as drab as the woman herself. But the distaste in them as they studied Mallory was vivid enough. "You are with Mr. Carella?" she asked, and Mallory realized that the woman had a slight accent.

"No, I had a six o'clock appointment with Mr. Mills. I'm Mallory King."

"When you were not here at the correct time, we thought you were not coming," Myra murmured.

"I wouldn't have made it without Mr. Carella's help. My car's down the road, stuck. I hope Mr. Mills will still see me."

"Do come in while I go up and tell Mr. Mills you are here," she said in her oddly annunciated English.

Mallory was thankful not to be sent away, and she turned to tell Tony goodbye for the second time. But he simply stepped past her and into the house. His coat brushed her arm, and the fleeting feeling of his body heat barely materialized before he was past her. A shiver came involuntarily, then she stepped inside, making sure to keep some space between herself and Tony.

In the glow of three massive chandeliers that illuminated a vast entry foyer, she got her first good look at Tony. In a long, dark overcoat parted to show a pale shirt and charcoal slacks, the man looked as big, dark and intense as she remembered from the theater. And the edge she felt then was still firmly in place. But now it seemed that it was touched by a certain nervousness that he hadn't shown before.

She didn't understand him—not why he was at the theater, on the road in the storm, or in this house with her—and she averted her eyes from him. She chose to look at the foyer, with its natural stone walls that soared up through three stories and had carvings of horses fashioned into the hard surfaces. As Myra closed the door and shut out the night, Mallory looked up at the heavily beamed ceiling, then down to the reflected light from the chandeliers on polished black marble floors.

A sweeping staircase to the right was framed by intricately carved banisters and turned posts twined with boughs of holly, and it led up to a second-floor balcony. Twenty-foot-high doorways, both right and left, arched over carved wooden doors, and the air was touched with the pungency of woodsmoke, lemon wax, pine and a lingering cool dampness. A Christmas tree decorated with crystal globes and golden garlands looked oddly formal sitting directly opposite the front doors. A simple star topped it, and white linen swaddled its trunk, spreading out onto the black marble.

"I will be right back," Myra said as she went past Tony and Mallory and headed for the staircase. Her low-heeled shoes clicked against the hard floor.

When Myra reached the top of the stairs and went to the right through an arched opening, Mallory turned to Tony. "You didn't have to come inside with me."

"Of course I didn't," he said as his dark eyes narrowed on her. "Tell me, what do you think of all of this?"

She shrugged, wishing she could get out of her damp coat and away from him. He made it difficult to focus on anything when he was this close to her. "It's incredible. I think I read in a magazine or something that Mr. Mills built it, but it looks as if it's been around for centuries."

"Some of it's new, some of it's old. This is part of the original house, probably built a hundred and fifty years ago by one of the area's great vintners. Then Mills took over the estate about forty years ago and started tearing out vineyards to make room for expansion, from extra wings to stables and guest cottages. He even had stones from a quarry in Ireland shipped over for the newer construction. In all the time he's been here, he's never stopped construction."

He looked around the area, his dark eyes roaming over the vast foyer. "He believes that if he quits building, he'll die."

# CHAPTER THREE

Mallory knew her mouth must have dropped. "He really believes that?"

Tony cast her a slanted look. "I don't think he *really* does, not anymore than I believe the place is haunted."

"It's haunted?"

"I've never actually seen a ghost, but there are stories about night wanderings and strange happenings."

She looked for a hint of humor in his expression, but there was none, just that brooding sensuality that made her feel slightly off-balance. "You're kidding, aren't you?"

He motioned to the area with one hand. "Doesn't this place conjure up ideas of strange things going bump in the night? Even the new parts—the south wing that's being built right now—supposedly has had incidents that can't be explained. A perfect atmosphere for hauntings, I'd say."

The house definitely was different and a less-than-homey place. As she looked at Tony, she had the passing thought that he really looked as if he fit here, in a place of dark shadows and strange happenings. And his words were making her nerves even worse.

"That's ridiculous," she muttered to stave off the uneasiness that prickled at the back of her neck.

"You don't believe in things you can't see, that can't be explained?"

She'd retreated into the world of make-believe for a lot of her life. That was probably why she went into acting, taking whatever parts she could just to be able to create illusions and magic on the stage. And it had helped her survive foster homes and loneliness after her mother died. But right now she wanted reality and facts. She wanted this job. A chill in the air brushed her face and made her shiver.

"What I believe is that I'm cold and damp and probably not going to get my meeting with Mr. Mills."

A flash of movement at the top of the stairs drew her attention, and she glanced up to see Myra standing by the top newel post, fingering a holly leaf. For some reason she had the feeling that the woman had been there, just watching, choosing her time to move and draw the attention of the two of them.

"Mr. Mills will see you now in his suite."

Mallory was relieved that the man wasn't just turning her away. "That's great."

The woman flashed Tony a glance. "Perhaps you can tell William where Miss King's car is, and he can take care of it?"

"Of course," Tony said.

"And your luggage?"

"My car's right out in front. Everything's in the trunk. The key's in the ignition."

Mallory frowned at Tony as a part of the riddle of this man became clear to her. "Mr. Mills is the busi-

ness associate you were talking about in the car, isn't
he?''

"As a matter of fact, yes."

"You never said."

"There's a lot you didn't say, too," he murmured,
a certain tightness touching his expression.

Strangely, she felt as if he had duped her someway,
and she turned from him to go to the stairs. As she
took the steps one by one, she could feel Tony watching her, the way she could at the theater, his eyes bor-
ing into her back.

When she reached the top of the stairs, she chanced
a look back down into the foyer. But the space was
empty. Tony had vanished as quietly and completely
as if he had never been or as if he were a ghost. She
could still feel the tingling in her wrist where he'd
touched her in the car, and she shook her head as she
turned to follow Myra through the arched doorway.
The man certainly wasn't a ghost.

As Mallory followed Myra into a broad hallway, she
pushed the ideas of ghosts and hauntings out of her
mind and focused on what lay ahead of her. The interview with Saxon Mills.

She went down the hallway, past closed doors on
either side, which were heavy wooden barriers set into
stone walls and were partially covered by faded tap-
estries. Thick Persian carpeting underfoot muffled any
noises, and gas lanterns wired for electricity were
spaced every twenty feet or so, casting a yellow glow
over everything.

The chill Mallory had felt in the lower level was
more pronounced up here, and the mustiness of age

that had only been hinted at in the foyer was stronger. Mallory followed the housekeeper to the end of the corridor, where highly polished wooden doors barred the way. Without knocking, the woman pressed an ornate latch and opened the doors. With a glance back at Mallory, she motioned her to follow her inside.

Mallory stepped into a dimly lit room that matched the rest of the house perfectly. It looked as if it occupied one of the turrets, with a domed ceiling overhead, multi-angled stone walls and heavy plank flooring partially hidden by individual Persian carpets and runners. A massive fireplace set into the wall to the right had five-foot-tall marble horse statues at either side, rearing into the air.

The fire in the hearth radiated welcoming heat, and the dancing flames reflected off the polished surfaces of furniture that, even to Mallory's untrained eye, were obviously priceless antiques. In the center of the room was a huge sleigh bed set on a marble platform that raised it ten inches above the floor.

Mallory turned to speak to Myra by the door, and came face-to-face with a man who she didn't have to be told was Saxon Mills. Tall at about six feet, he had a wiry leanness to him, and thick, snow-white hair brushed back from an angular face. In a bloodred smoking jacket, dark slacks and leather slippers, he stared at Mallory with deep blue eyes partially shadowed by shaggy brows.

He didn't speak as he came closer and slowly circled her, looking her up and down as if she were livestock to be bid on. When he came back to face her, he asked in a rough, well-used voice, "Your coat?"

Mallory quickly slipped off the damp coat, and the housekeeper came forward to take it from her.

"Myra, bring Miss King some hot tea," the man said without looking away from Mallory. "And prepare dinner to be served at eight sharp. Tell the others to be punctual."

Silently the housekeeper turned and slipped out of the room, and Mallory heard the door click shut after her. Thankful for the feeling of warmth from the fire at her back, she said, "I'm sorry I'm late."

"You're here," he said quickly.

"Yes, I am."

"I was sorry to hear of the accident last night at the theater."

Obviously, Henry Welting had been near the theater when it happened, or perhaps this man had read it in the paper, the way Tony had. "It was pretty terrible."

"The girl who was hurt, is she—?"

"Sara is still alive," Mallory said quickly. "She's holding her own, but she was badly hurt."

"Good," he murmured, dismissing that subject with a vague brush of his hand. "Now, something else. Myra tells me that you came here with Tony."

"Yes, I did. My car went off the road and he came along, thank goodness." She could sense tension in the man, and after what Tony had said about him, she wondered if the feelings were mutual. Business associates who hated each other? "He rescued me, gave me a ride here."

"Henry Welting was supposed to make very sure that you didn't discuss this meeting with anyone. I trust that you didn't discuss it with Mr. Carella."

What they had exchanged hardly qualified as a discussion. "Of course not. I just told him I had an appointment with you."

His eyes narrowed. "Nothing more?"

"Not really."

"What *did* you tell him?" he bit out.

For some reason she didn't tell him about the meeting at the theater. She didn't know why, but the words just never came. Instead she said simply, "He knows I'm an actress."

"You told him why you were meeting with me?"

"No, I didn't. I just said that I had to be here by six to see you. That's it. I didn't give him any details at all. I wasn't about to. He's a stranger. I didn't even know he knew you until we got here."

He was obviously relieved. "Henry was quite right. You'll do perfectly."

Mallory barely contained her own relief. "You still want me for the part?"

"Absolutely. Henry said that you agreed to the two-week run, so I think, all things considered, this will work out quite well." He moved away from her to cross to a marble-topped table and two leather chairs positioned by the fireplace. "Come," he said as he took one of the chairs. "Sit. We need to talk."

She didn't have to be coaxed to go closer to the warmth of the blaze in the hearth. She took the chair opposite Saxon Mills and watched him settle, resting his elbows on the padded arms.

As he steepled his fingertips, he peered at Mallory. "I have it on good authority that you are a very good actress. Are you also a quick study?"

"In fact, I am," she said as she settled in the warm leather. "I never have trouble learning lines."

"Good. There's a lot of information you'll have to remember to do this job correctly. And I expect a top-notch performance from you."

"I'll do my best, but I haven't even seen the script yet."

He flicked that away with the wave of one hand. "It's not needed."

"Excuse me?"

"There is no script. This is a rather…unique role—improvisation of sorts."

"Mr. Mills, I don't understand. Mr. Welting said you wanted me as a replacement for another actor. I assumed—"

He stared right at her, his cold blue gaze stopping her words. "Rule one, Miss King. Don't assume anything if you work for me."

*Everything and everyone is expendable for Saxon Mills.* Tony's words echoed in Mallory's mind, and she could feel the tension in her neck and shoulders coming back full force. She needed this job, no matter how uneasy this man made her. Tony worked with him, probably making lots of money, and he didn't even like him. Pressing her fingers into the soft leather of the chair arms, she tried to keep her gaze level. "Of course. Why don't you explain things to me."

He lifted one eyebrow. "That's exactly what I was about to do."

She bit her lip, not trusting herself to say anything else, in case she said the wrong thing again.

"I don't know how much you know about me, but you need a brief background. I am a self-made man. I was born in relative poverty, one of two sons of immigrants, and I promised myself I would never be poor again—no matter what it took. That's how I've lived my life. I get what I want, and I won't take no for an answer." He tapped his forefingers together over and over again as he spoke. "This house is mine. There isn't another like it anywhere. One of a kind. Very unique."

So was the man speaking. "It's a remarkable house."

"That's when you know you're successful, Miss King, when you have something that no one else has, something that no amount of money can really duplicate. And it's worth what it takes to get it." He was silent for a moment, his blue eyes unblinking. "Do you understand that concept?" he finally asked. "Do you see the kind of man I am?"

No wonder Tony didn't exactly like him. Saxon Mills was obsessed with Saxon Mills. "Yes, I think I do."

He shifted the subject abruptly. "Henry told me that you've done a lot of stage work."

"Mostly small theater."

"Why do you work on stage?"

"I love live theater. You feel as if you're really living the part when you hear reactions immediately."

"Excellent. How do you feel about lies?"

She was beginning to feel a bit like Alice in Wonderland just after she fell down the rabbit hole. Nothing was making sense—from meeting Tony again on a rainy road in the storm, to sitting here opposite a man who wouldn't have a problem taking the part of the Mad Hatter. "I don't understand."

"Lying, as in not telling the truth? Lying for a valid reason, without feeling remorse or regret?"

She shrugged. "I suppose acting is a lie. You take over a part, and you pretend that you're another person for as long as the curtain's up. You have to make people believe you're that person."

"Exactly," he said with a sigh. "And that brings me to the reason you're here. I have a part for you that's one of a kind. It's unique, and I'm sure it will be very demanding."

"What *exactly* is the part?"

His hands dropped to the arms of the chair and his long fingers smoothed the leather. But his blue eyes never left her face. "Before I tell you, you have to agree that no one will know anything about it except you and me, and that it will go no further than this room and the two of us."

Madness on top of madness. "If I'm on the stage—"

"You won't be."

She stared at him, her heart sinking. "You said I could have the part."

"And you shall."

"Mr. Mills, the request to come here was a bit odd, but I agreed to it because I was under the impression that this offer was legitimate. I'm serious about my career.''

''And you're serious about getting more money for this job than any that you've had so far in your fledgling career.'' He sat forward and she found herself pressing back into the chair to keep the distance between them intact. ''Every job you've had, you've done for next to nothing. Most were insignificant roles, walk-ons at best, or parts in plays that were run on goodwill and the ridiculousness of people who would work for meals or the sound of applause.''

A feeling akin to hate rose in Mallory as she stared at the man. He had no qualms about cutting people down with words. She didn't have a clue how she was going to walk away—would she find Tony and beg him to drive her out of here?—but she wasn't going to stay in the room with this man. As she started to stand, he stopped her with a sharp command.

''Sit down. I'm only trying to reach an understanding with you. I guarantee you, Miss King, this is a legitimate offer. It's a very sensitive issue, for reasons you'll understand when I explain everything to you. Just give me your word that even if you walk out the door in the next five minutes, you won't tell anyone what went on in here.'' He drilled her with his eyes. ''Anyone.''

She knew her position was tenuous at best. Her car was stuck, and this place was out in the middle of nowhere. And if she were honest, the last thing she wanted to do was get back in a car with a man who could upset her equilibrium with a single look. Leaving wasn't a viable option at the moment.

"Okay," she said. "I agree to that."

"Excellent."

"What is it you want me to do?"

"I want you to play the part of my daughter for the next two weeks."

Mallory sat very still, not sure she'd heard Saxon Mills correctly. "Excuse me?"

"I thought that was pretty straightforward," the man said, his tone laced with barely concealed irritation. "I need someone to assume the role of my daughter for the next two weeks."

"Mr. Mills, I—"

He held up one hand. "Call me Saxon. I don't think Father or Dad would be terribly convincing at the first."

"Are you doing an autobiographical play or something?"

That actually brought a smile to his face, but it didn't touch his eyes. "No. This is no play. It's my life." He sank back farther in the chair and his eyes narrowed. "It's a matter of life and death for me." The words sounded melodramatic, but his face was contained, almost cool.

A knock sounded, and as the door began to open, Saxon leaned toward Mallory and whispered, "Say nothing of this in front of Myra."

Mallory nodded and sank back in the chair. While the housekeeper laid a tea service out on the table, Saxon Mills spoke with her. The word *mad* came to mind, along with *crazy* and *demented*. Play his daughter? The idea was so absurd that Mallory almost laughed.

As Myra went to the hearth to stir the fire into new life, Saxon nudged a cup of tea across the table to Mallory. "Drink it while it's hot. You'll be glad for any warmth you can find in this house during weather like this."

Mallory had totally forgotten about the storm and the dampness in her slacks and her sodden shoes. Myra moved quietly for being such a large woman. She silently crossed the room, and the door clicked shut behind her. Mallory reached for the tea and cautiously took a sip, letting the hot liquid slip down her throat and settle in her middle, easing her tension just a bit. But as soon as she looked at Saxon over the rim of her cup, her nerves tightened again.

The man was staring at her, but she had the idea that he wasn't really seeing her. His gaze was slightly unfocused, as if he were lost in a place of his own making. "It's quite remarkable," he murmured softly.

"Excuse me, sir?" Mallory said as she lowered her cup, cradling it in her hands on her lap.

He flinched, then took a harsh breath and reached for his cup of tea. "We need to discuss this job."

"Yes, we do. It's all so rushed. I was only contacted last night by Mr. Welting. If I had more time, I could do a better job for you."

"We only located you a few days ago, and we needed to be sure you were right for this part. As for doing a good job, being spontaneous will probably only enhance your talents."

For a moment she thought he was trying to flatter her, but one look at his blue eyes and she knew he was just giving her an answer. "How can I pass for your daughter when anyone who knows you would know your daughter and know I'm obviously not her?"

"That's the beauty of this idea. I don't have a daughter. Everyone knows that. So you don't have to *be* anyone but yourself. They won't have a clue what to expect, because they won't know you exist until I introduce you to them. As far as background goes, I've been briefed on yours, and it fits perfectly."

She frowned. "You said they know you don't have a daughter. Where am I suppose to have come from?"

He stood and crossed to a night table by the bed on the marble pedestal. Despite his age, he moved easily, Mallory thought, and when he came back to the table, he held out an eight-by-ten gold picture frame. "This should explain things a bit."

She put her cup back on the table and took the heavy frame from him. A sepia-toned studio photo was set in it, an ethereal-looking picture of a delicately beautiful woman with feathery dark hair framing a heart-shaped face, large dark eyes and pouty lips. The image startled Mallory, and she blinked. Her memory had to be playing tricks on her.

"Who is this?" she asked as Saxon took his chair again.

He sank back, watching Mallory. "My Kate," he said with a sigh. "And you look a lot like her, Mallory. A lot."

She looked at the picture again, hating the way the memories of a five-year-old child were overlapping with it. But when she really looked at the picture, she knew her mind had played tricks on her. This woman wasn't really like the mother she remembered. This woman, maybe in her early twenties, looked delighted with life and was openly flirting with the camera.

Mallory had no memory of her mother smiling or being happy. What memories remained were scattered and few, of a sad, bitter woman beaten by life. A woman who had died too young.

"Kate?" she asked, looking at him instead of the picture.

"She's a woman I knew almost thirty years ago. I was mad for her, but we were both too stubborn, too volatile, probably more in lust than in love. It just burned out after six months, and she left to get on with her life."

His tone was unemotional, as if the memory of the incident with the woman had little lasting effect on him. Yet he'd kept her picture all these years.

"Henry Welting was astounded when he saw you. You look so much like Kate did at one time. It would be very easy for anyone who's seen Kate's picture to believe you could be a child from our affair, that Kate was your mother."

Bitterness burned at the back of Mallory's throat. She quickly put the picture down flat on the table, and Saxon sat forward to reach for it. Without a glance at it, he turned it facedown on the table in front of him.

"Did you have a child with her?" Mallory asked, her voice sounding tight in her own ears.

"I have no children. But you're a good enough actress to make people believe it could be true."

"What happened to . . . to this Kate?"

He didn't blink. "She died years ago in Europe."

Again no emotion. And that made Mallory feel even more edgy. It didn't help that the storm went unabated, crashing around the stone walls and tearing at the night outside with lightning. "Who's this charade for?"

His expression tightened. "My family, Mr. Carella, the staff. Everyone who's in this house for the holidays."

She wondered if this was all some horrible practical joke the man was setting up. "Why would you want to deceive these people?"

"That's something that's complicated and personal, but I can give you a general idea. I have little family, just a niece and nephew. My only brother's children. Warren has been gone ten years, but he left his son, Lawrence, who's thirty-two. He calls himself a writer, but from what I can see, all he writes is IOUs and bums around being 'creative' while others pay for it.

"He sees me as the way to finance his dilettante lifestyle. Then there's Joyce, his sister. She's married to Gene Something-or-other. I believe he's husband number three. I can't think of why he married her except he's a patient sort who's willing to wait until she gets her hands on my money."

He sighed. "I'm fed up with them, but one or both of them will be my heirs. I've never been married, so, as shabby as they are, they're the only blood relations I have."

"What good would it do to pretend you have a daughter for two weeks?"

He steepled his fingers again and began to tap his forefingers together. "Maybe no good at all. Or maybe a lot of good. Maybe if they think you're my direct heir, they'll get on with their lives without waiting for me to die so they can celebrate. Maybe it would help me sift out the wheat from the chaff, so to speak."

Mallory had little experience with family in her life, but it seemed that Saxon Mills didn't have a great deal more, despite all his wealth. "I'm sure they aren't just sitting around waiting for you to die."

"Of course they are," he said without rancor. "So are Myra and William."

She frowned. "William?"

"Myra's son, a stupid man who seems to think the way to do anything in this world is through brute force."

"Why would they want you gone?"

"Myra's been with me for years, and I'm sure she thinks she and William will make out quite well when I'm gone."

Mallory watched the man and knew she wouldn't make a bet on his generosity to anyone. "What about Mr. Carella?"

"Tony's a bit different, more dangerous. He's greedy like the others, but he's got brains. He'll do whatever he needs to do to get what he wants, and he doesn't worry about the consequences."

The words sounded strangely similar to what Tony had said about Saxon. "What does he want?"

"He's been involved in some of my businesses for ten years, and he's here to talk me into letting him buy me out." He exhaled. "Or maybe he wants me to put him in my will so he gets control of my shares when I die. One way or the other, he wants control of the businesses, come hell or high water."

She was uneasy about underestimating Tony, about thinking he could be easily deceived. The man could look at someone as if he could see into their soul, and if she was going to lie to him, she'd have to be very convincing. "Can he get control?"

"He's got the brains and a strong instinct of when to go for the kill, but he's up against me. He only gets it if I say he does."

She could tell this man enjoyed that power. "So, you'll tell all of them you found an heir and they're out of luck?" she asked, her tea growing tepid as she listened with morbid fascination to the man's twisted plans.

"Exactly. I want to throw a monkey wrench into their plans and get them off my back. If they think I found a long-lost daughter, the product of my foolish liaison years ago, maybe they'll leave me alone for a while." He paused, then added, "Maybe it will bring out the true colors in all of them. All the better for me to make a decision."

Mallory sat forward. In a distorted way, this meeting was like a scenario that had gone through her mind over and over again through the years. The moment in which she would find the man who'd walked out on her mother, that he would admit he was her father and would hold out his arms to welcome her into his family.

That was fantasy, a self-delusional lie. Yet she couldn't help but think that if Saxon Mills really was her father, she would be just as apt to walk out and keep going. He clearly liked people to dance to his tune. He played with people, manipulating them for his own purposes. He didn't even come close to any idea she had of what a father should be.

"That's the bare bones of the plan," Saxon said. "Now, tell me what you think about it."

"I don't know what to think. I suppose you must feel your reasons are compelling for you to go to all this trouble."

"Yes, they *are* compelling. Will you do it?"

The fire crackled and popped, and Mallory could hear the storm beating against the windows behind the heavy velvet drapes, but she never took her eyes off Saxon Mills. No matter what his motives were for this deception, the role was simple. She knew she could do it. She didn't have to like him, or even approve of what he was doing. All she had to do was keep up her part of the agreement and leave in two weeks with enough money to keep her going for a while.

"Well?" he prodded, and she could hear the tinge of impatience in his voice.

She made an instant decision. "I'll do it."

# CHAPTER FOUR

"Excellent," Saxon murmured, then levered himself out of his chair and crossed to the bed. "Remember, outside the walls of this room, you are in character, and you stay that way. No talking about any of this, not even to me, unless we're in here." He looked back at her, his hand hovering over the raised nightstand. "You're my daughter. I'm your father...unless we're in here. Understood?"

"Yes."

He pressed a button on the nightstand, then turned back to Mallory. "I'll have Myra take you to your room now."

She stood. "Don't you need to tell me more about all these people I'm supposed to be deceiving?"

"Why? You just came here tonight and found out you're my daughter. You wouldn't know much about me, and even less about my family and acquaintances."

"What if they ask questions about my life? What do you want me to tell them?"

"Tell them the truth as much as you can. Tell them you work as a waitress, that you live alone, that you don't have any other family."

She knew her jaw must have dropped a bit. "You had me checked out, didn't you?"

"I had to. I know your mother died from pneumonia when you were five, and you were in various foster homes until you were old enough to escape the system and go out on your own. You have two years of college as a drama major, and you've worked as a waitress to help support yourself so you can act." He ticked off her life with an ease that shocked her. "You've had roommates, but you've lived alone for the past six months. You're twenty-eight years old."

"All right. I get the idea." She looked at the photo that was still facedown on the table. "What about her...Kate? What do I tell them about her, since she's supposed to have been my mother?"

"Tell them the truth about your mother, except for the fact that your mother wasn't Kate. Tell them what you remember, what she was like, and leave it at that. And she died in Europe."

"My mother never even made it out of California as far as I know, let alone Europe."

He waved that aside with a sharp jab of his hand. "Then don't talk about her death. As a rule of thumb, stick to the truth as much as possible, and when you need to add details for authenticity, play it by ear. Your own clothes will be fine most of the time, but there are a few things in your room for you to wear when you need to be more formal. There are riding clothes, just in case you want to ride when this storm is gone."

It was a bit unnerving to think someone had purchased clothes for her, but she knew that her casual jeans and sweaters weren't exactly a full wardrobe. "How do you want me to play this part?"

He looked genuinely taken aback by the question. "Why, as if you're my daughter, someone I just found, and someone who just found out about me."

He didn't have a clue that she had no idea how to relate to a father. Robert King had been nothing to her but a person her mother talked about very rarely. "I meant...am I happy to be here, or angry, or disturbed?"

"Ah, I see." He fingered his chin as he obviously considered the question. "I know that my family is going to see you as an interloper, possibly a gold digger, so I suppose we should give them what they want. You're thrilled that I'm wealthy, that you don't have to work anymore. That you can have everything you ever wanted and then some. Oh, one more thing."

"What's that?"

"I want you to tell me about anything any one of the others says to you about me or my businesses. I think a daily report is in order. Let's say we do lunch up here every day from noon to one, and you can fill me in on what's going on."

A knock sounded, and Saxon looked at the door as Myra silently entered the room. "Myra, show Mallory to the blue room."

The woman glanced at Mallory, then turned without a word and left. Saxon crossed to where Mallory stood by the table and leaned toward her to speak in a whisper meant for her ears only. "I'll see you at dinner." He actually smiled, but the expression looked more predatory than friendly. "At eight o'clock the curtain goes up and the fun begins."

The next moment, Saxon stood back and spoke in a normal voice. "Go and settle in, then I'll come and escort you to dinner just before eight. And wear the blue dress."

Mallory nodded. "I'll see you just before eight," she said as she turned and headed for the door. When she stepped out into the corridor, she found Myra waiting. Myra turned and led the way back to the foyer balcony, then across and into another corridor that ran at an angle back from the front of the house.

Myra stopped by double doors at the end of an arched hallway and opened the right-hand door. She stood back to let Mallory step into a room that had to be part of a turret, too. It had the same configuration as Saxon's room, but on a less-grand scale, with no pedestal for the poster bed and, instead of a fireplace, a freestanding stove that glowed with heat.

Where dark richness had dominated the man's room, in this space the angled stone walls were covered with floor-to-ceiling wooden panels, carved horses inset on each one. The furniture was more delicately fashioned, done in pale wood. The windows were draped with rose chintz, and the bed that stood in front of them was covered with an ice blue eyelet spread topped by a bank of lace pillows.

Mallory turned and spotted her luggage standing by the door as Myra said, "William brought your things from your car. Everything is in the dresser or the armoire. Your toiletries are in the bath." She pointed to a closed door to the right of the armoire. "There are plenty of towels in the cupboard under the vanity, and hot water is plentiful."

It made Mallory feel strange to know that this woman had gone through her things, but she said, "Thank you."

"Do you know how long you might be staying with us?"

"I'm not sure, but I'll be here for the holidays."

The woman stayed by the door, not making a move to leave. "If there is anything I can do to help you, just ring the bell by your bed."

"I will," Mallory said, wishing the woman would leave, but Myra didn't seem ready to budge.

"Your car will be taken care of when the storm lets up a bit. William locked it and the key is in the drawer by your bed."

This woman could make a person feel suffocated, even when she seemed to be helping. "Thank William for me."

"Of course. Dinner will be served in the main dining room. At the bottom of the staircase, go right, and—"

"That's okay. Saxon is going to show me down."

Myra's mouth tightened at Mallory's use of the man's first name. "They dress for dinner here," she murmured, then slipped out and closed the door.

Mallory exhaled, relieved to finally be alone, and she threw the old-fashioned bolt on the door before the woman came back. Then she crossed to the armoire, opened it and found her sweaters and blouses hung neatly from perfumed hangers, side by side with clothes she'd never seen before.

There were three dresses, two short and one long, with matching shoes lined up perfectly on the shelf underneath, next to her worn running shoes and casual boots. All the dresses were probably worth more money than she saw in one year. A black sequined sheath, a deep blue crepe with a scooped neckline and cap sleeves, and a full-length strapless dress done in ivory silk, with a narrow waist, deep V front and an indecently low back.

Saxon had said the blue. She fingered the crepe, the fabric so delicate under her fingers that she was almost afraid of tearing it. "They *do* dress for dinner," she said quietly as she took out her cotton bathrobe and closed the door.

She stood by the radiating heat of the stove and stripped off her damp clothes. As the warmth touched her bare skin, she sighed. For the first time all day, she felt a degree of relaxation. She glanced at a digital clock on the table by the bed and saw she had over an hour before she had to begin the role. A hot bath sounded wonderful to her.

Laying her clothes over a chair by the stove to dry, she slipped on the robe, but as she started to pull it around her, the hairs at the back of her neck tingled. She turned quickly, the sense of being watched so strong that she expected to find Myra there eyeing her with her cool condescension. But the door was shut, the bolt still thrown and the room empty.

She scanned the room as she tied the belt of her robe at her waist. She was alone, but Tony's words about haunting and ghosts had obviously worked on her. "Stupid, foolish," she said out loud, her voice echoing in the high-ceilinged room. "There are no ghosts. There are no ghosts. There are no ghosts."

Yet even as she said the words over and over again as she headed for the bathroom, she wondered if she would open the door and see someone standing there with their head in their hands. She didn't realize she was holding her breath, until she opened the door, flipped on the light and found the room empty. She sighed with relief.

She looked around the white, blue and gold-accented room. It was lit by a teardrop chandelier suspended from a domed ceiling over a massive claw-foot tub sitting in the middle of a cold, white marble floor. Light bounced off of mirrors that lined the walls, and flashes of the storm invaded the room through round windows set along the bottom edge of the ceiling. Rose-colored towels had been set out on an expansive vanity along the wall to the left, and a hint of roses touched the air.

As Mallory stepped into the room, the chill of the marble under her bare feet, she thought the room looked like something out of a fairy tale. A tower for Rapunzel or Sleeping Beauty. Fairy tales came in dark versions, too, and Mallory had the most uneasy feeling that if she blinked wrong or turned quickly, she'd see someone . . . something.

Quickly, she closed the heavy door and wished that she hadn't listened to Tony's stories. She didn't need help to get her imagination going on strange tangents.

She turned on the water for the bath, thankful to see it steam into the air as it rushed out of the gold-plated faucet. While the tub filled, she crossed to the vanity and looked at her own reflection bouncing back at her a myriad of times in the mirrors that surrounded her.

She smiled wryly, knowing that she didn't look as if she belonged here any more than Saxon Mills looked as if he could be anyone's father. With her eyes smudged from weariness, her hair curling wildly from the rain, setting off paleness in her cheeks, she looked more like a waif than a long-lost heir to the Mills fortune.

That thought stopped her. That's exactly what a child of Saxon's would be. Someone who would literally take the money of inheritance—billions, according to Tony—out of his hands and the hands of Saxon's family. And the control of businesses out of Tony's hands. She grimaced as she shrugged out of her robe and hung it on a gold peg on the door. A spoiler, that's what Saxon Mills wanted, and she'd hired on for the part.

After turning off the water, she stepped into the steamy comfort of the tub. As she sank down to her chin, she closed her eyes and rested her head against the curved porcelain.

*They dress for dinner.* Myra's words conjured up an absurd image of unwitting people going to Saxon Mills's table naked and getting beheaded by the king.

Laughter born out of tiredness and slight hysteria bubbled up in her. But it stopped abruptly when she thought of one of those people being Tony. An image of him naked came to her with startling clarity, his skin sleek and tawny, his shoulders broad, his body lean and hard, an arrow of hair on his chest, darting downward....

Heat that had nothing to do with the water rose in her and she opened her eyes quickly. She was used to her fantasies, dreams that had kept her going during her life, but to have a teenager's daydream about a man who was almost a stranger was absurd. "That's enough," she told herself as she sat up and rested one arm on the edge of the tub. "More than enough." But the images of Tony lingered until she tried to deliberately think of something else.

Mallory started to sink back down in the water, feeling an easing in her, until a chill in the air brushed her skin. With jarring suddenness, the sensation of being watched was there again. The unsettling sense of being the object of intense scrutiny. It was so overwhelming that Mallory instinctively crossed her hands over her breasts and twisted around to look at every angle of the room.

But she didn't see anything except her own reflection bouncing back at her over and over again in the mirrors. Then, as suddenly as the feeling came, it was gone. She knew she was totally alone. Slowly she sank back down in the tub and forced herself to breathe deeply and evenly. Whatever she felt had vanished, just as Tony had when she'd looked back down into the foyer earlier.

When Saxon came for Mallory at five minutes to eight, he was wearing a formal tuxedo. The man looked elegant in the finely cut suit worn with a pleated white shirt and diamond studs down the front. His white hair, groomed back from his gaunt face, was a perfect complement for the blackness of the tux.

He stood in the doorway, eyeing Mallory slowly up and down, the way he had at their first meeting. She was wearing the deep blue dress, the softness of the material lying lightly on her skin. The gathered gauzy skirt brushed her legs with each step she took, and the neckline was just low enough to expose a suggestion of her breasts. She'd never worn such an elegant dress in her life, nor one so expensive.

Saxon inclined his head to her and murmured, "Almost perfect," then held out his closed hand to her. Slowly he opened it, palm up and said, "This will make it stunning."

Mallory looked down at a single, perfect sapphire surrounded by diamonds, blazing incredibly blue against his skin, with a chain that was so fine, it was the merest suggestion of silver.

"It's beautiful," she whispered.

"It's one of the most perfect sapphires in the country, and the diamonds are blue-white and set in platinum." He motioned her to turn and he helped her put it on.

Its cool weight rested just above her breasts, a sensuous sensation she'd never experienced before, and she turned to Saxon. "How does it look?"

"Perfect. You're the image of Kate," he whispered, offering his arm to Mallory. "Curtain time, daughter."

She rested her hand in the crook of his arm and walked in silence beside him down the stairs, across the foyer and past the Christmas tree. They went under the balcony toward the back of the house. At the end of a short, broad hallway, Mallory saw Myra standing by a massive arched doorway.

The woman's eyes were averted as Mallory and Saxon went past her and into a formal dining room area that was more of a grand hall. From the top of two steps that led down into the room, Mallory had an overall impression of the long room with its muraled walls, vaulted ceiling, glittering crystal overhead and massive, dark furniture.

Several people were gathered around a dark trestle table decorated with poinsettia arrangements, but the only one she saw clearly was Tony, who was standing by one of the high-backed chairs. In a dark jacket, with a gray shirt done up to the neck and no tie, he seemed lean and dark. The edge of sensuality she'd felt from the first wasn't diminished by his distance or the table that separated them. And she knew it was going to take all the skill she had to get this deception past him.

Saxon urged her down the steps and onto a floor fashioned from sheets of gray slate. "Good evening," Saxon said as they approached the head of the table. "We have another guest for the holidays. Mallory, you know Tony already," he murmured.

"Yes, of course," she said, looking at Tony without making direct eye contact.

As she looked at Saxon, she saw him motion with his free hand to a woman sitting at the table. "Joyce, my niece," he said.

The woman sat rigidly in the high-backed tapestry chair. Everything about her seemed red, from her coppery hair twisted into a severe knot at the back of her head, to the velvet gown that only emphasized her heavyset figure, to what looked like rubies that glittered at her ears and throat. As she stared at Mallory, she nodded stiffly, but didn't say a thing.

"Joyce's husband, Gene Roseman." The man next to Joyce was probably fifty. His brown suit looked as if it fit him badly, and his thinning gray hair was tousled around a ruddy, bearded face. He looked at Mallory with undisguised boredom, then muttered, "Hello." Without waiting for her to respond, he reached for his wineglass.

"And Lawrence, my nephew," Saxon said.

The man sitting opposite Gene and beside Tony looked as if he were in his early thirties. With jet black hair cut at a fashionable length, high cheekbones, a deep tan, a chiseled jawline, clear blue eyes and a lean build set off by a white silk shirt open at his throat, he looked as if he'd stepped out of an ad in a gentleman's magazine. He stared at Mallory, not bothering to hide his obvious shock at her appearance or bothering with any pleasantries.

He put down his wineglass with a cracking sound that echoed in the room. "What in the hell is going on, Uncle?" he demanded.

"I was just about to tell you, Lawrence. I want you all to meet Mallory King." Saxon paused dramatically, then finished with, "Mallory is my daughter."

If there had been a collective gasp, Mallory couldn't have felt the shock in the room any more clearly. She knew Tony was staring at her, and the others were sitting in stunned silence. For what seemed an eternity, no one said anything.

Then Joyce finally asked, "Your *what?*"

"My daughter." Saxon covered Mallory's hand on his arm with his own hand. "I wanted her to come here so I could get to know her better...and for her to meet her family." He moved back from her, breaking contact to turn and look at her. "You've all seen the pictures of Kate. Don't you think she's the spitting image of her?"

Myra had come into the room with a compote of fruit and had all but frozen, staring at Mallory and Saxon. Gene looked up and frowned. "What's he talking about?" he muttered.

"Kate," Joyce said. "A woman he had an affair with years and years ago."

"I thought Kate just haunted *you,* Uncle, but it looks as if good old Kate has come back to haunt all of us this time," Lawrence said with biting sarcasm. When Mallory looked at him, he was smiling, but the expression never touched his eyes. "I never really believed in the ghosts...until now."

"Don't be so stupid, Lawrence," Joyce said, flashing him a sharp look. "This isn't a joke."

"It certainly isn't," Saxon said, urging Mallory to the chair at his right by the head of the table. With the heat from the fireplace at her back, she settled on the tapestry seat, then glanced across the table where Tony was taking his seat.

When she looked at him, she expected shock and anger. She knew he'd see her as a barrier to him getting his hands on Saxon's part of the businesses. And God knew how much of a liar he thought she was after the ride they'd shared and all the evasions she'd handed him. But when she met his gaze, she knew he wasn't surprised at all.

She quickly looked away as the thought that he'd known about her all along came to her. But what did he know? Had he heard about the plan and shown up at the theater to check her out? He couldn't know that this was all a lie, or he would be on his feet to denounce her. But Saxon made it clear that only he and Henry Welting were in on the ruse.

If Tony had somehow heard the scheme before this announcement, before *she'd* known, that would explain why he'd come to the theater to check out Saxon Mills's long-lost heir. And if that was the case, he was as much a liar as Saxon was . . . and as she was.

She looked down at her hands, pressed to the snow-white linen on the table. One way or another, he wasn't saying anything yet. So, for the moment, she was Saxon Mills's daughter, a woman who each person in this room would wish off the face of the earth . . . including Tony.

Tony could feel the shock and anger that vibrated in the huge room, and he watched the little drama unfold with Mallory in the center of it. Even Myra seemed off-balance, scurrying out of the room without making a sound. When he'd been told that the old man had a daughter, he'd been stunned. The thought of Saxon Mills having progeny was unsettling at best. But when he'd come face-to-face with her at the theater, he'd been unprepared for his reaction to her.

He'd gone backstage to try and get closer, but he hadn't counted on her running directly into him. He hadn't counted on eyes the color of sapphires looking up at him, or feeling her delicateness under his hands. The person who could destroy what he'd worked for for the past ten years was the image of a woman dead for almost thirty years, a woman who turned Saxon's world on its ear. And Tony knew Kate's child could do the same thing to any man.

The Ghost of Christmas Past? She was haunting him right now, and everyone else at the table. He watched her closely as he sipped his wine, welcoming the warmth trickling down his throat. The woman was a part-time actress, a waitress as poor as a church mouse, and she came to find the Mills's fortune. When she glanced at him, her lashes veiled her eyes, not quite hiding an uneasiness in her gaze.

She was nervous as hell, and she had every right to be. If emotions could kill, the emotions at this table would annihilate her on the spot. He sipped more wine, and he knew that he should pay a bonus to the person in Welting's office who had forewarned him about Mallory's existence.

Lightning crashed outside, and the white light penetrated the room with a ghostly glow, touching Mallory with a paleness that accentuated the deep blue of her eyes. For a moment he could believe she was a wraith, an illusion, the ghost that Lawrence spoke of. Then thunder rumbled outside the stone walls, the light faded, and Mallory lifted her goblet to her pale lips. The glimpse of her delicate wrist reminded Tony of her silky heat under his fingers when he'd touched her in his car.

No, she wasn't a ghost. The world was out of balance, but this wasn't a haunting. She was a part of

Saxon Mills. And as much a game player as her old man. Anytime during the ride to this house, she could have told him who she really was, but she'd chosen to give half answers and partial lies.

He was weary of dealing with Mills, and the old man's games. Now he had to deal with his daughter. And since Mallory King had made it into this house, she was the enemy. Everything Tony had—and would have—depended on him keeping it clear that she was someone to be removed from this picture.

It didn't matter that the deep blue dress clung to her curves and the swelling of her breasts, or that the color only intensified the deep hue of eyes that echoed Saxon's. Then he saw the glitter at her elegant throat, and he felt as if he'd been struck in the gut. She was already getting into the family fortune, wearing a hundred-thousand-dollar necklace as if it were a paste bauble. He looked away as Lawrence spoke.

"All right, Uncle, when are you going to tell us the punch line?" Lawrence was asking, his elbows resting on the table.

"You've heard my punch line, Lawrence." Saxon glanced at Myra as she returned to the room to present a bottle of estate wine for his approval. "Fine, Myra, perfect," he murmured, then looked back at Lawrence as the woman tipped the bottle to pour a trace of the deep red liquid into his crystal goblet. "And she is no ghost. Mallory is very real…and very permanent."

Myra's hand jerked unexpectedly and the deep red wine splashed onto the pristine whiteness of the tablecloth. "I am sorry, sir," she murmured, quickly sponging at the spreading stain with a cloth from her pocket. "So sorry, sir."

Saxon barely reacted to the incident, an unusual occurrence since he normally used any opening he had to harangue the woman. Instead, he tested the bouquet of the wine, then took a sip into his mouth and closed his eyes as he ran it over his palate.

As he put down the goblet, he murmured, "Pour, Myra," and looked at the people sitting at his table. "These holidays will be our time to establish a family."

Tony watched Lawrence studying his uncle, and in a fraction of a moment, Tony saw Lawrence literally shift his expression from annoyance and anger to something that could only be called ingratiating. "Of course, Uncle. Family. The most important thing in the world. Blood ties."

Good old Lawrence. A known quantity. If you can't fight them, kiss up to them—the man's rule of thumb for existing in the Mills family.

"Family is everything," Joyce murmured as she looked at Mallory, her annoyance displayed openly in the set of her jaw and the way her hands clenched on the white linen cloth. "Family and breeding."

Lawrence and Joyce were Tony's enemies, but totally known and totally controllable. The comments about family and blood ties were two-edged coming from them, since their own mother had been a secretary in the company offices when their father had married her. Now Mallory had been tossed into the mixture, and he felt as if he'd been pushed back to square one.

"Breeding?" Lawrence snorted as he glanced at Tony, then back to Joyce. "Sister, sister. None of us at the table want to get into that, do we?"

Joyce flashed him a cutting glance. "I just meant that we don't know anything about Mallory... except that Uncle says she's his daughter. I'm just interested in some details, that's all."

"We all know what you're interested in," Lawrence countered.

"So, Tony," Saxon said, ignoring his niece and nephew with an ease he'd perfected over the years, "what do you think?"

He glanced at the man. "About what?"

Saxon reached to touch Mallory's hand where it rested on the tablecloth near the deep wine stains. "Why, Mallory, of course. My new family."

Tony fingered the coolness of the crystal goblet and kept his eyes on Saxon. He wasn't about to look at the woman again. It was that much simpler to think clearly without having to meet her blue gaze directly. "What about her?"

"How do you feel about meeting my daughter?"

There was no way he could explain his feelings since he'd first laid eyes on Mallory King at the theater. "I'm shocked. She never gave me a hint about her real identity when I found her."

Joyce all but choked on a sip of wine she'd been taking, and stammered, "You... you *found* her?"

Saxon spoke up quickly. "Her car went off the road about a mile from here, and Tony happened upon her and helped her out by driving her here." He stared at his wine, swirling it slowly in the expensive crystal goblet. "As far as what she said or didn't say on the ride, Mallory and I had already agreed to keep this news just between the two of us until we met face-to-face."

Tony cautiously eased his gaze over to Mallory, bracing himself, but he was relieved to find her looking at Saxon. "Actually, I was talking about when I first met her while she was playing a ghost, the Ghost of Christmas Past. I didn't know at the time that her haunting would be in the present."

# CHAPTER FIVE

Tony watched Joyce sputter out her wine, Lawrence jerk his expression toward him, and Myra stop laying out salad plates to stare at him. But it was Saxon's reaction that said the most. Mallory hadn't told him about the theater meeting.

Tony could see the way the old man's hand tightened on Mallory until she frowned. And it was obvious she would have pulled away if Saxon hadn't held it so tightly. But Saxon didn't look at Mallory. "What are you talking about, Tony?"

"Coincidence. I was at the theater and there she was, all swaddled in white, wearing holly in her hair and haunting Ebenezer Scrooge, much the same way Kate seems to have haunted you."

Saxon glanced sharply at Mallory, his hand still holding hers. "What is he saying?"

"He was at the theater. That's all." Her voice was low and husky, the tone playing havoc with his nerves as she looked right at Tony, as if daring him to say more. "We barely even talked. I didn't know him, and he didn't know me. I just ran into him—literally— when I was trying to get onstage."

"You're an *actress?*" Joyce asked, with the same inflection she would have used for a prostitute.

Mallory moved her hand away from Saxon's and reached for her wine. As she cradled the goblet in her hand, she slowly rotated it back and forth and met Joyce's stare. "I've had a couple of small parts, and I work as a waitress. I've had a lot of jobs."

Joyce almost snorted. "A waitress *and* an actress?"

Tony watched bright color stain Mallory's cheeks, but he had to hand it to her. She didn't back down from Joyce at all. She looked right at the woman and said, "It's honest work, and I support myself."

Joyce waved one hand in dismissal. "Well, I'd say you can forget that—the starving actor bit and all—if you really are Uncle's daughter. You've found your own personal pot of gold."

Tony expected Mallory to counter that, but she didn't. She took her time sipping the wine, then looked at Joyce and said without apology, "I guess so. I heard Saxon had millions. Now I find out he has billions." She cast Tony an even look, reminding him of his own words in the car. "I'd say I found my treasure at the end of the rainbow."

Only the buffer of the massive table between them kept Tony from throwing his wine in her smug face. How could a woman go from delicately vulnerable to hard and grasping in the beat of a heart? He sat back. "Rainbows are an illusion," he murmured, "not something to count on."

She lifted one finely defined eyebrow in his direction. "The only thing I count on is Saxon. He found me and brought me here. I didn't come looking for him."

The wine that cost a fortune was turning to vinegar on Tony's tongue. Looking away from Mallory, he asked Saxon, "How did *you* find her?"

Lightning crashed outside, vibrating the glass in the windows as Lawrence leaned toward his uncle. "Yes, do tell us how this miracle happened."

The man flashed Lawrence a look that would have withered anyone except his nephew. "You all know I've been working on my business affairs. Setting things in order. And I realized that a loose end from the past needed to be settled once and for all. I never put an end to the period of my life with Kate. She left suddenly, and there never was a satisfactory ending to any of it."

"I'd say being dead is pretty much an ending," Lawrence said.

"It is, but I never knew exactly what happened to her. I had Henry Welting check on it for me, and he found that Kate had a lot of problems after we broke up. She made a hasty marriage that didn't last, and she was quite sick during the last years of her life. But he also found that she had a daughter nine months after she left me."

Mallory startled Tony when she spoke up again. "My mother died when I was five years old."

Gene, who had sat there silently during the conversation, finally spoke up. "Didn't Saxon say your last name was King?"

"It is. Saxon told you that my mother got married just after they broke up. I thought that man was my father. He left us when I was an infant, so I don't remember him, but I did have his last name."

"Who brought you up after your mother died?" Lawrence asked.

"I was in foster care, but I've been on my own since I was sixteen."

"Being an actress and waitress," Joyce muttered.

Mallory wasn't having any trouble getting into this part. She used her own background and embellished when she had to, slipping into the part of the poor destitute woman who found a rich father with an ease that startled her. With these people to play off, she felt reactions that she didn't have to fake. Right now she wondered if it would be in character to get up and slap Joyce's smug face. "Is that a crime?" she asked.

"Joyce just has a hard time relating to anyone who actually works for a living." Lawrence shrugged. "She always has been in the dark when it came to any form of physical labor."

"I work," Joyce snapped. "I've got my charities and I have—"

"Is that what you call Gene nowadays?" he asked smugly.

Joyce barely acknowledged Myra, who had finished pouring the wine and had begun to silently ladle soup into delicate china bowls at each place. "Well, am I the only one here who finds it incredibly fortuitous timing for a long-lost daughter to come waltzing through the door?"

Mallory glanced at Saxon and could see a gleam in his eyes. He was enjoying this infighting and didn't bother to try and mask his pleasure. He really was a game player, a master manipulator, and everyone in the room was dancing to his tune...except Tony. She looked at him sitting back in his chair, observing everything from hooded eyes, his expression unreadable. He'd been silent since the comment about pots of gold and rainbows.

But Mallory wasn't fooled. She knew Tony was just waiting for his chance to blindside her. She could almost feel the tension radiating from him.

"Timing is everything," Saxon murmured.

"It certainly is, especially when you're revising your will," Joyce muttered.

"His will?" Mallory asked.

"As if you didn't know." Joyce lifted an eyebrow in Mallory's direction. "He told us we were supposed to be here for the holidays so he could tell us exactly what the terms of his new will are."

Joyce glanced at Gene, who sat there like a bump on a log, totally disinterested in anything that was going on outside the soup he was eating now. "Gene and I were invited to Aspen by the Birchfields, but we canceled our plans at the last minute to come here."

Mallory stared down at the soup Myra spooned into her bowl, the deep brown steaming liquid shimmering back the overhead lights. The old man was everything she thought. Bring in a bogus daughter and get everyone at each other's throats. Then choose the winner. The fantasies she'd had about a family were so far from this reality that she realized she was relieved she didn't have any blood ties to these people.

"The lure of finding out just what you'll have to squander on Gene's stupid business ideas was just too much for you to resist, wasn't it, sis?"

Joyce glared at her brother. "I don't have to sit here and take this from you, Lawrence."

"Then leave."

"Don't you wish," she muttered, and determinedly turned to Tony. "Didn't he ask you here to discuss his will?"

Mallory was more than aware of Tony clenching his hand around the wineglass. And she was surprised that the fine crystal didn't break. He was angry, but holding that anger under control, probably by sheer willpower. "No. I'm here to convince Saxon to rethink his allocation of business control if something happens to him."

"In plain English, you want to make sure that our uncle doesn't give up his power to anyone but you," Lawrence said.

"That's your translation, not mine," Tony murmured, releasing his grip on the goblet. He flexed his strong, square-tipped fingers on the white tablecloth, and his eyes never looked away from Lawrence. "A warped translation."

"Maybe, but I'd bet my life you didn't expect him to pull a daughter out of his hat? A direct heir. Someone to snatch all that power right out from under you."

Tony stared at the man, a muscle in his jaw working, but he didn't say a thing. Lawrence shrugged sharply, then spoke to Saxon. "You could have saved us a trip in this storm," he muttered.

Mallory stared down into her soup bowl, the thought of eye contact with Lawrence making her skin crawl, and the idea of eye contact with Tony out of the

question. The man unsettled her, and she needed to get
what control she could.

"So, Mallory," Lawrence said directly to her. "How
did you find out about your old man?"

She picked up her spoon and slowly stirred the
steaming soup. "Henry Welting contacted me." She
chanced a look at Lawrence, who was ignoring his
soup completely, opting for draining the last of his
wine. "Mr. Welting asked me to come here to meet
with Saxon."

"Where did Henry Welting find you?"

"San Francisco," Saxon cut in, saving her from
having to respond. "She's been there all this time."

"Acting and waiting on tables," Joyce said with
dripping condescension. "So now you're playing at
being the loving daughter?"

Mallory forced herself to stay in character and not
let the words that accidentally laid out the truth shake
her. Instead, she smiled at Joyce. "I don't have to act
that part," she said, dropping her soupspoon as Myra
began to clear the bowls. "It's a reality.

"Well, if Henry Welting hadn't stumbled across
you, Uncle would have never known he had a daughter, would he?" Lawrence said. "And you'd still be
waiting on tables and playing the part of a ghost."

"As Saxon said, Lawrence, timing's everything."
She lifted her wine goblet, thankful her hand was
steady. "Here's to timing."

"Here's to greed," Lawrence murmured before he
drained his drink.

Mallory let her gaze skim past Tony, who didn't
move, to Saxon, who held his glass up. "Here, here,"

he said, touching the rim of his goblet to Mallory's. "And also, a toast to my newly found daughter."

Mallory sipped the mellow wine as she glanced around the table. Joyce was flushed with anger. Gene didn't stop eating. And when she looked at Tony, she wished she hadn't. His dark gaze was on her, unblinking and unnerving.

As the storm raged outside, Mallory felt the rage in Tony. The room seemed filled with negative energy, and when she lowered her gaze to the plate of food Myra slipped in front of her, her stomach clenched. She wanted to scream at Tony to stop it, that she could deal with the others, but not him.

She wanted out of here, to a place where she could be alone to regroup. She glanced at Saxon as she pushed her plate away. "I'm sorry, Saxon. I'm so tired. I think I'd like to go up to my room." She laid her napkin by her untouched food and pushed back her chair. "Besides, you all need to talk."

He rose as she did and looked genuinely disappointed that she was removing herself from the little scenario he had so masterfully created. "Are you sure, my dear?"

"Yes, very," she murmured. She glanced around the table, not focusing on anyone, least of all Tony. "It's been a long, hard day. It was a pleasure meeting all of you. Good night," she murmured as she turned and headed for the door.

Once out in the hall, she waited for the door to shut behind her, then she exhaled with relief. She was tired. That was the truth, but she felt tense. Sleeping wasn't something that would come easily for her in this place.

She crossed the marble floor, but before she got to the sweeping staircase, she veered off toward a room on the far side. The doors were open, and she looked into a shadowy space barely touched by the lights in the foyer.

She could tell it was a library, maybe thirty feet by thirty feet, with twenty-foot ceilings and shelves filled with enough books to service a small town. Three walls were hidden by the heavily laden shelves from floor to ceiling. A full bar was set into the shelves to the left, and a fireplace directly across from the door was laid for a fire, but unlit. The room felt decidedly chilly.

She moved farther inside, then turned on a side light near the heavily draped windows on the front wall. The low glow was enough for her to see the leather-bound books interspersed with pieces of art. When thunder crashed outside, Mallory moved to the window and tugged the heavy material back enough to expose leaded windows. The glass was distorted, hiding details, but the impression of darkness and storm was clear.

Mallory shivered as a chill teased the bare skin of her arm, and as she let the fabric fall from her fingers, she turned. She barely covered a gasp of shock when she came face-to-face with Tony two feet from her, silently watching her. She had no idea how long he'd been there. She hadn't heard a thing. She pressed a hand to her chest, and her heart pounded against her palm. "You scared me."

He shrugged as he pushed back the sides of his jacket to thrust his hands in the pockets of his dark slacks. "At least you didn't hit me in the middle this time."

She put her hands behind her back, not wanting to think about that moment of impact in the theater, that mingling with heat, strength and maleness. "What are you doing in here?"

"Why didn't you go upstairs?"

"I hate that."

"What?"

"Answering a question with a question."

He shrugged again. "I hate not getting answers to my questions."

She wasn't up to fencing verbally with Tony. She knew to survive she had to be sharp, and she certainly wasn't sharp right now. "I came in to look at the books. Why are you in here and not at dinner?"

"I lost my appetite." He glanced at the shelves, then back at Mallory. "Did you know that most of the books in here are first editions?"

"I don't think I've ever seen a first edition of anything but a newspaper."

He almost smiled, his rueful expression playing at the corners of his wide mouth. And Mallory found herself wishing he'd really smile, so she could see if it would touch his eyes and mellow out the darkness there. "These books are worth a hell of a lot more than a quarter."

She turned from him and went to the shelves that framed the doorway. She touched the spine of the nearest book with the tip of her finger, the fine leather etched with gold writing. She tried to make out the title in the low light. "*The Essays Of A President.* I've never heard of it."

"Not too many people have. Especially not—"

She turned to him, cutting off his words. "Especially not a waitress and struggling actress?"

"I didn't say that."

"You thought it."

He met her gaze. "Do you read minds, too?"

"It's not too hard to figure out where you're coming from."

He rocked forward on the balls of his feet, the action somewhat intimidating, and Mallory had to fight the urge to move even farther from him. "That should make things simpler all-around."

"I guess so." She moved away from him, past bookshelves with titles that were lost in shadows. But her attention never left Tony, even as she stopped by a shelf on the back wall that held an assortment of exquisite bronze sculptures of horses. All were about ten inches high, and even in the dim light she could make out the beautiful, painstaking detail. She touched the cool metal of the nearest piece, tracing the foreleg of a rearing stallion with the tip of her finger.

"Your father has a fixation with horses." Tony spoke from close behind her, and it startled her. He must have been following her as she moved around the room. "He only keeps a few in the stables right now, but he's never without some."

She glanced at the other statues. "They're lovely."

"They're originals by Mandalay."

She'd never heard the name, but his tone let her know they were probably priceless.

"Do you have a clue what they're worth?" Tony asked.

She drew her hand back from the cool bronze and turned to find Tony within two feet of her, the white lightning through the window flashing behind him. For that split second he was all black, stark and horrifying, like some demon. Then the lightning was gone and the dull softness of the side lamp threw him back into a blur of shadows.

"I..." She touched her tongue to her cool lips and wished she'd eaten something. The wine was bitter in her stomach and a headache was beginning to form behind her eyes. "No, I don't. But I am tired." She started for the arched doorway.

"Mallory?"

Tony didn't touch her, but the sound of him saying her name was enough to stop her before she stepped out into the foyer. "What?" she asked without looking back at him.

"Don't you want to know why I followed you out here?"

She stared into the warm light of the foyer, an escape that she couldn't use. "Why did you?" she asked softly.

"To get something straight."

The headache began to throb in earnest at her temples, and she closed her eyes for a moment before she made herself turn to Tony. "To get what straight?" she asked.

He'd moved to the door with her and the lights from the next room touched his face, making deep shadows at his jaw and throat. "It's pretty obvious the only reason you're here is because of Saxon's money."

He'd hit the nail on the head, but not in the way he thought. "What are you—a mind reader?" she asked, mimicking his own tone from moments ago.

"I don't have to be. You weren't exactly hiding the fact in there that you're pleased with your father's wealth."

She was uneasy to have him so close, but angry enough at his attitude to grab at that anger and use it as a defence. "Wealth? You're the one who said he had billions. Why wouldn't I be pleased? You would be, too, if you had to decide if you were going to ride to work, or walk and use your gas money to buy day-old bread and a jar of peanut butter."

He stared at her hard, but she knew her words didn't have any effect on him when he reached out and flicked the sapphire at her throat. His finger skimmed coolly over her skin in the process, and she barely concealed a shiver. "I think that's worth enough to buy peanut butter for a decent-size country."

She pressed a hand over the pendant and glared at Tony. "It's not mine. Saxon just let me wear it to...go with this dress."

"A dress his money bought?"

"I'd tell you it's none of your business, but I'd lay you odds that wouldn't stop you."

"You'd win. I know you think you found your fatted calf, the goose that laid the golden egg, but you're dead wrong."

Her head was pounding now, and she was having trouble focusing on Tony. His image was blurring slightly in front of her, yet that wasn't all bad. At least it eased the sharp edges in his expression as he looked down at her. "All I think I found is a father."

"Siring a child doesn't make a man a father."

It hadn't made her real father a father. He was never any more than a man who walked out and never came back. "No, it doesn't." She pressed her fingertips to her temples and slowly rotated them to try and ease the pain. "You said you were going to tell me why you followed me in here. Is this it? To give me some sort of lecture on fathers and money?"

He moved even closer to her, making the room seem claustrophobic despite the high ceilings and rambling space. A mellow after-shave clung to him, mingling with a scent of maleness that seemed to be everywhere, a scent that intensified her headache. "No."

She lowered her hands and narrowed her eyes. "I'm not going to play guessing games. It's late and I'm tired, and I'm going to go up to bed."

"All right. I want to know what it would cost me for you to disappear."

Surely the headache was making her hearing muddled. "What are you—?"

"How much?"

"This is ridiculous."

His expression tightened. "Didn't you learn anything in that dining room? Do you think Joyce and Lawrence are waiting with open arms to welcome you to this family, to let you get Saxon's estate?" His laugh was harsh and jarring. "After what went on in that room, I'd say you'll be lucky to get out of here alive."

"Stop it," she hissed.

"One thing you can count on with the Mills family is that they don't give a damn about anyone besides themselves. And they'll do anything they have to do to keep what they've got or get what they want. Saxon's right at the top of that list."

"How about you?" she found herself asking, unable to stop the words. "What would you do to get what you want?"

"Whatever it takes," he said without hesitation.

This was getting out of control in a big way and she had to stop it. "I'm not leaving. I just got here."

"Would one hundred thousand dollars change your mind?"

The wine rose bitterly at the back of her throat, and she had to swallow hard. "What?" She barely recognized her own voice, a tight, faint sound in her own ears.

"A hundred thousand dollars. Right now. No one needs to know."

She'd taken this job for the money, and she was playing the part so well that this man wanted to give her a fortune to disappear. She knew she should laugh at the absurdity of the whole situation, but she couldn't. Not when the cut-and-dried bribe made her feel as if she'd been struck in the middle.

He wanted her out of the way, gone, dissolved into thin air. He wasn't any better than Joyce or Lawrence, and maybe even worse, because she sensed that he had more substance to him than either of them had.

"Well?" he asked, obviously impatient to get an answer.

"Sorry. You can't buy me off for a hundred thousand dollars," she muttered.

"Then name your price to disappear from this place and Saxon Mills's world for good."

Everyone in this house was mad, from Saxon Mills right down to Tony. There was no "family and friends" here, just deceit and greed. Disgusted, she turned from Tony to leave, but he caught her by her upper arm before she could take a single step.

She jerked free of his touch as she spun to face him. Anger burned in her, and she suddenly realized the anger came from hating him for trying to buy her off, but also because a part of her wanted him to not be like the others. But he was...just like them. "You don't have enough money to buy me off," she grated, hating the way her eyes were beginning to smart.

His expression tightened. "Saxon can throw you out on your butt if he decides that you aren't the daughter he wanted, and you'll be lucky to leave with a hundred pennies."

"Everything boils down to money for you, doesn't it?"

Unexpectedly he reached out and flicked her chin with the tip of his finger, the contact astounding her with the way it made her whole being tense. "It does for all of us. Think over my offer. It won't be good forever."

Without another word, he turned and strode out of the room. She could hear his feet striking the marble floor, then the sound was gone, and all that was left was the storm that beat around the stone walls.

Mallory scrubbed the back of her hand across her chin where Tony had touched her last. "Damn you all," she muttered, turning to go out of the library into the deserted foyer.

She started up the stairs, and just as she stepped out onto the balcony and started in the direction of her room, another bolt of lightning struck. It turned every visible window into white energy, with thunder following it immediately, then the lights in the foyer flickered and died.

Mallory grabbed for the railing of the balcony as she was plunged into darkness, but at the same time she felt the cool wood under her hand, the lights flashed back on. She waited, almost holding her breath, but when they stayed on, she turned and hurried across the balcony into the hallway that led to her room. When she was a few feet from the closed door to her suite, lightning struck again.

Thunder overlapped the jolt of energy, and in the next instant, the lights flashed once, then flickered out and died. Mallory didn't move. She waited in the complete darkness, hoping for the lights to come back on, but they didn't. Blindly she reached in front of her, took a cautious step, then felt for the door with her hand.

She felt down the sides of the panel, found the knob and twisted it. The barrier creaked slightly as it swung back, and the low fire glowing dully through the grate on the stove gave enough light for Mallory to orient herself and figure out exactly where she was going.

She stepped inside, closed the door, then crossed to the stove. As she reached out to hold her hands toward the low heat, she was startled by the rasping sound of a match being struck behind her. She spun around, barely covering a gasp when she saw Myra standing near the door, carefully lighting a candle.

# CHAPTER SIX

When Myra shook the match to put it out, she looked at Mallory. The flickering of the candle flame played across her stoic face, turning her eyes to black pools, and Mallory released a breath.

"Myra, you startled me. I didn't hear you come in."

The woman held the candle holder a bit higher. "I thought you might need this."

"Thanks," Mallory said, then she glanced at the door and remembered the creak when she'd come in. But there hadn't been a sound before Myra appeared.

As the woman swept past Mallory toward the bed, she said, "Storms play havoc with the power. There have been lightning strikes around here before and the power was out for days."

Mallory watched Myra set the candle on the nightstand by the bed. Then she turned, the candlelight at her back, her face in deep shadow. "William went down to the stables to check on the generator." She motioned with one hand to the small table by the heavily draped windows. "I brought up your dinner. Mr. Mills thought you might find you were hungry, after all."

Mallory glanced at a tray with two silver-covered plates on it sitting on the table. Myra had been in the room before Mallory ever came in. That answer made sense, yet Mallory was uneasy because she hadn't sensed the woman behind her before she struck the match. "Thank Mr. Mills for me," she murmured.

"I shall." Myra didn't make a move to leave. "May I say something, miss?"

"Go ahead."

"I was here when your mother was with the mister."

"You knew Kate?"

"I was here when he brought her into this house, and I was here when she left."

Mallory was curious. "Why did she leave?"

Myra shrugged. "They were always fighting. That night it was stormy, like tonight, and they fought into the wee hours of the morning."

"Do you know what they fought about?"

"No. I just know your mother left." It was impossible to see her eyes in the low light, but Mallory knew she was staring at her. "She wore blue that night, the way you are tonight, and she wore that necklace. She threw it off the balcony."

Mallory cringed. Rationally, she knew this was all a costume, a way for Saxon to create his own ghost. But it made her skin crawl to know he'd made her a real clone of Kate, and she had to force herself not to snatch the sapphire off her throat.

"For the longest time, the mister forbade anyone from speaking her name."

Even knowing about the man's games, Mallory couldn't help but feel a twinge of sadness that whatever had been between him and Kate had died such an ugly death. "She never came back here, did she?"

"No, she never did," Myra said flatly. "It was almost as if she had never existed . . . until now."

"I guess my being here isn't a very comfortable thing for the family."

"It is a very difficult thing for everyone in this house," she murmured. "And it will be difficult for you, *very* difficult."

She couldn't fight the truth of that. "I suppose it could be."

"Rest assured, it *will* be," she said darkly, then, without another word, she turned and went to the door. As she left, the door hinges creaked softly, then the latch closed with a solid click. Mallory walked to the door and threw the bolt, then fumbled with the clasp on the sapphire pendant and slipped it off.

She stared at the gem lying on her palm, the flicker of the candle catching its brilliance in the dark blue and the fire of the diamonds that framed it. Kate's necklace. She should have expected that, but it didn't make her feel any less ghoulish wearing it. She closed her fingers over the coolness of the pendant, then turned to cross and strip off the dress. But a sharp rap on the door stopped her.

She didn't want to see anyone else tonight, but she couldn't pretend she wasn't in here. "Who's there?"

"Joyce."

Mallory closed her eyes for a moment. The last thing she wanted was more of what Joyce seemed intent on dishing out. "What can I do for you?" she called through the wooden door.

"I need to speak to you," Joyce said, her voice almost a hiss.

Reluctantly, Mallory slid the bolt back and opened the door. Joyce didn't wait for an invitation before pushing past Mallory. "Close the door."

Mallory didn't have any fight left in her right now, and the headache was making her vaguely sick. Just get it over with, she thought as she swung the door shut and turned to find Joyce over by the stove, her hands held out to capture what heat there was. "You should have had Myra relay the fire for you before she left." She cast Mallory a glance. "You aren't used to servants, of course, but you can't let them get the upper hand."

"I don't even like the word *servant,*" Mallory muttered.

Joyce shrugged. "Hired help, then. Is that acceptable to you?"

"Employee."

"Whatever." Joyce rubbed her forearms with the flats of her hands. "This place is like a tomb. Cold all the time, winter and summer. It never gets warm enough."

Mallory didn't intend to indulge in chatter with this woman. "What do you want, Joyce?"

"A talk with my cousin."

Mallory moved to the bed and sank down facing Joyce. She rubbed at the ache between her eyes with the tip of her forefinger. "All right. Just say what you want to say."

The woman studied Mallory for a long moment. "I don't think, even if you'd grown up in this family, that we could have been close."

"No, we probably couldn't have." Mallory wondered if anyone could be close in this family.

"That doesn't mean that I can't offer to help you."

Mallory's hand stilled on her forehead, then slowly lowered to her thigh. "Help me? How could you help me?"

"I can give you some advice that might help...under the circumstances."

Mallory exhaled, clenching her hands on the fine gauze of her dress, and she felt the pendant bite into her palm. There was no curtain going down in this play, no clean-cut distinction between the acts when she could rest and catch her breath. It just went on and on and on. "What advice?" she muttered.

Joyce moved to stand over Mallory. From her crossed arms to her slightly lifted eyebrow, her whole demeanor was condescending. "First, don't get too used to all of this. It's transitory, subject to Uncle Saxon's goodwill. I know that better than anyone."

Mallory didn't say a thing, but the woman didn't seem to care. She kept talking and went off on a tangent.

"Do you know why I married Gene?"

Mallory shrugged, certain it wasn't for his personality or good looks. "No, I don't."

"Because he's the only man I ever got involved with who wasn't threatened by Uncle Saxon. He just doesn't care. The others saw it as a battle. Gene sees it as something that happens and brushes it off."

"Smart man," Mallory muttered.

"No, adequate."

"Did you come in here to talk to me about your marital state?"

Her expression tightened. "No, I came up here to do you a favor."

"And what's that?"

"I think you should leave before Uncle Saxon decides to throw you out."

She shook her head. "What are you talking about?"

"He discards people, Mallory. Just the way he gets rid of anything that ceases to be useful to him. He threw your mother out when he decided that he was tired of her."

"They fought and she left."

"She was thrown out, lock, stock and barrel. When Saxon tires of something or is disappointed in something, he gets rid of it. From what I heard, Kate was a major disappointment, and she was yesterday's news in the blink of an eye. And so will you be. If he found out something about you that was distasteful, you'd be out. It wouldn't matter what blood ran through your veins."

Joyce wasn't here to buy her off the way Tony had tried to do, but it was just as ugly. "If you're trying, not so subtly, to tell me that you're going to try and blackmail me into leaving, forget it. You can't tell Saxon a thing about me that he doesn't know already." She stood. "Don't threaten me, Joyce."

The woman didn't back down, but Mallory could see the hint of uncertainty in her expression. "I didn't threaten you. I was just trying to help."

"I don't need your help."

She exhaled on a hiss. "You're a fool. You didn't find a father, you found a master, and a cruel one at that."

"Joyce, that's—"

"And if you think what I've I told you is hard to take, wait until Tony turns on you. He's a pro." Mallory knew her eyes must have widened, because Joyce almost smiled. "Yes, Tony. I saw the way you were looking at him in the dining room."

Mallory knew that heat was beginning to creep into her cheeks. "What are you—?"

Joyce flicked that away. "He'll take you apart. He's not going to look at you, fall head over heels for you and back your claim. It doesn't matter what you think."

Mallory hated the idea that this woman had seen something in the dining room, something that she'd thought she'd hidden. "I know what Tony is. He's as greedy as the rest of you," she said with real distaste.

"As greedy as you are, but he's got the muscle to back it up."

"He's got money, I know that."

"He's got connections."

"I know Tony's involved with Saxon's businesses."

Joyce eyed Mallory, obviously measuring the words before she said, "I wasn't talking about those connections. I was talking about who he is."

"Oh? Just who is he?"

"I don't know if waitresses watch the news or read the papers, but surely even you've heard about Joseph Danforth."

Mallory frowned. Of course she'd heard about Danforth. Five years ago, his name had been all over the news, splashed in the headlines and in the tabloids—a businessman who had been arrested for tax evasion and been convicted after a lengthy, expensive trial. The last she'd heard he'd been in prison, and the rumors of his gangland ties were dying down.

"Of course, I've heard the name," she said.

"Then you heard that he was mixed up in some heavy dealings with pretty unsavory people, people who usually get rid of any people who get in their way?"

"There were rumors about mob involvement. I just don't understand what this has to do with Tony."

Joyce almost smiled, as if she were enjoying every moment of this. "Everything. Joseph Danforth was Tony's father."

The candle flickered from an errant breeze, and Mallory felt the bite of the precious jewelry in her hand as her fingers clenched around it. "Tony is Danforth's son?"

Joyce narrowed her eyes on Mallory. "His *only* son."

She shook her head, not wanting to think about those subtle feelings she'd experienced around Tony, that sense of him having a dangerous edge. "That's crazy. Tony's not even named Danforth."

"Wouldn't you change your name if you were trying to build a so-called legitimate business life and live with a certain degree of anonymity?" She shivered slightly. "If I was you, I wouldn't be alone with the man. Goodness knows what he considers 'persuasion' when it comes to business dealings."

The memory of his touch came back with such force that she had to make herself not touch her arm where he'd captured her. "And people lie about things," she breathed.

"This isn't a lie, cousin. The man's the last of the Danforths and every drop of blood in his veins is Danforth blood."

"Saxon knows all of this?"

"Of course. Ask him about it." She dismissed that with a sharp shrug. "I suspect he enjoys dealing with the man, living on the edge, so to speak, and thumbing his nose at the conventional business world. Besides, Saxon's every bit as cutthroat as Tony is. They're two of a kind, cold and calculating and capable of destroying people on a whim."

The candle flickered again, and a deep chill seemed to be creeping into the room. "It's getting late," Mallory said as she stood to face Joyce. "I need to get to bed."

"Sure. Just don't forget that I survived here, and I'm going to keep surviving. I won't let you walk in here and take what's mine. I might not have Tony's connections, but I've earned my place here."

"What *is* your place?"

"I belong here. You don't. It's that simple." She turned and headed for the door, but with her hand on the latch, she looked back over her shoulder at Mallory, who stood by the bed. "Remember, sooner or later, I'll get what's mine."

With that, she left, closing the door softly behind her. Mallory hurried across the room and threw the bolt again, determined that no matter who came to that door next, she wasn't opening it. She crossed to the armoire and let the necklace fall from her hand into a tiny drawer.

Taking off the blue dress, she found the long white T-shirt she used to sleep in, folded neatly along with her underwear. She slipped on the cotton shirt, and as it settled on her bare skin, she retrieved the candle from by the door and carried it over to the table.

So, Tony was the son of a gangster, a man shamed in public and left to rot in prison. That didn't square with the elegant clothes Tony wore or the way he seemed to belong in Saxon's company.

That thought took her aback. What better person to survive around Saxon but a man who was accustomed to using life and death measures to get what he wanted?

She put the candle down by a tray with two covered plates and a goblet of red wine. She lifted the covers and found chicken, vegetables, salad and rolls. Picking up a roll, she turned to look at the stove.

As she tore the roll in half and started to nibble on it, she realized Joyce had at least been right about one thing. She should have had Myra reset the fire before she left. The room was getting decidedly chilly. After taking a sip of mellow wine to wash down the dry bread, she crossed to the stove and found two small logs in a basket to one side. She put them in, and sparks shot up into the chimney as the logs fell into the glowing embers.

Once the logs caught, she stripped the bed of the pillows and climbed in between the cool sheets. Snuggling down into the bed, she sighed from weariness. For several minutes she lay there, listening to the storm outside, going over and over her conversations with Tony and Joyce.

One thing she knew for certain, the people in this house were damaged, drawn together by greed and held together by their mutual intention to get what they thought was theirs. A family. Mallory almost laughed at that thought. And what of Tony's father, his family?

She pulled her knees up to her stomach. She'd never felt as if she belonged anywhere, and she knew that if Saxon Mills really had a daughter, she wouldn't belong here, either. Everyone would hate her. She shivered and pulled the blankets higher. She didn't want to think about hate and families, the Saxons and the Danforths.

She felt chilly air against her face at the same time the candle flickered, danced, then went out. In total darkness, Mallory debated whether she should get up to find a match and relight it, or stay where she was and try to get warm. She closed her eyes, concentrating on the little warmth she felt, and knew she didn't want to leave this bed again for anything.

She snuggled farther down under the comforter and sighed as she felt her tension begin to seep away. Then, suddenly everything changed. Someone was there, in the room with her. She bolted up in the bed, straining into the silent shadows. "Who's there?" she asked.

There was nothing except the sounds of the storm outside. Clutching the comforter up in front of her as if it could be protection against the unseen, she strained to see and hear. The sense of a presence in the room was so strong it was almost tangible, and the crazy talk about ghosts refused to leave her alone.

"Kate?" she whispered, and felt foolish even saying the name.

The wind moaned outside as rain was driven against the windows, and the chill inside was bone deep and soul shaking. Mallory held so tightly to the comforter that her fingers began to tingle. Kate was Saxon's ghost, not hers. But it was her imagination that was refusing to let go of the notion that the woman was caught in these walls. That she'd come back for something.

Mallory forced herself to breathe evenly, and gradually, ever so slowly, the sensation of eyes on her faded until she no longer sensed someone or something was waiting in the shadows.

Certain she knew she was alone, she slowly sank down in the bed and stared into the darkness until her eyes began to burn. When she felt near normal again, she tried to relax. She let go of her death grip on the linen, and she worked on shutting out everything except the desire to sleep and get out of this madness for a while. Finally she felt her heart slow, her breathing become deep and even, and she slipped gently into a welcome sleep.

*  *  *

*To see her standing there in one piece, smiling at Saxon's side, had been a sickening sight. Someone had been hit at the theater, there'd been the feeling of impact in the car, then screams. Mallory King should have been lying on that city street in the rain . . . dead. But instead she was here claiming her birthright.*

*The Watcher's eyes, accustomed to darkness, could see better than others', and there was no trouble making out Mallory in the bed, her dark hair framing her shadowy face. Her breasts rose and fell under the comforter, her steady breathing the only sound beyond the storm sounds. The Watcher knew that if a person inhaled just right, they could catch a hint of her scent invading the room the way she had invaded this house and the lives of everyone here.*

*She was ruining everything, taking all Saxon had to give, and that thought only intensified the need to be rid of her. And the idea of getting her out of here as quickly as possible was an obsession. With trembling hands, the Watcher reached for one of the pillows and leaned toward Mallory.*

Mallory seldom dreamed, and when she had before, her dreams had been unformed and disjointed. But this dream was so real she could have been standing in the vast dining hall again, feeling the chill of the air and the hatred in everyone sitting there. She could almost taste the hate.

Then, one by one they stood—Lawrence, Joyce, Gene, Myra, Tony—and started for her. She knew she should run, that she should make her escape, but she couldn't move. They came closer and closer, then slowly they surrounded her, boxing her in, trapping her. The air thinned and the chant of "get out, get out" rang all around her.

She saw Saxon standing to one side, the smile on his face one of pleasure at what he'd caused. Then she felt a touch on her, a hand closing around her wrist, and she turned to see Tony holding her. He was her anchor, her salvation, and she whispered, "Help me."

"I'll take care of you," he whispered, and the next instant, he had caught her against him. For that fleeting moment, she knew a feeling of protection, of being safe. But it was shattered by terror when Tony clamped a hand over her mouth, shutting off her air and the scream that was ripping at her throat trying to escape.

Fear burned away any sense of good in her, and she fought against the pressure on her face. Tony was just like the others, wanting her gone, taking care of her the way his father would have taken care of any enemy. And that knowledge hurt in the most horrible way, intensifying her sense of aloneness, but she wouldn't let him do it to her.

She clawed at the suffocating pressure on her face, thrashing back and forth. Dizziness made her head spin, and her lungs were on fire. Then threatening blackness crept up on her, and she knew she was going to die. The last thing she understood was a gut-wrenching pain that Tony could hate her so much that he'd kill her. Then the blackness swallowed her up.

\* \* \*

*The Watcher drew back, fury about to explode inside, and the hands that held the pillow were shaking so badly they lost their ability to grip the cotton. The pillow tumbled to the floor as the Watcher leaned down over Mallory's still body. In the dimness there was no movement, then a slight fluttery rise of her chest.*

*She was alive. Relief mingled with the hatred. It had to be an accident. No murder. No investigation. An accident. The Watcher tugged the comforter back over her still form, letting it fall without touching her. It was really too bad she had come here as Kate's daughter. The Watcher moved back, never looking away from the bed. Too bad she had to die.*

*December 23*

Mallory realized she was alive, with air going into her lungs. Her head hurt and her throat was raw. But she didn't know if she was waking from a nightmare or regaining consciousness after almost suffocating.

She lay still, thinking that maybe everything had been a dream, including Saxon Mills, this house and Tony Carella. But as she cautiously opened her eyes, she wasn't in her apartment in the city. It wasn't a dream. She was in the bedroom, where silence and shadows touched quiet orderliness.

She was on her back in the bed, with the comforter neatly laid over her, a pillow under her head. She blinked and slowly raised herself on her elbows. Nothing. Yet she'd never had a dream that real, that terrifying. She shivered as cold, damp air brushed her skin where the comforter slid down.

Tentatively she touched her face, expecting it to be bruised and sore, with her lips swollen from Tony pressing his hand there. But there was nothing. She sank back and stared above her at the shadowy ceiling. A dream. A nightmare, yet so real.

She looked at the bedside clock, but the digital screen was blank. She shifted and reached for the small light by the bed and snapped the switch. Nothing happened. The electricity was still off. Slowly she pushed herself up and swung her legs over the side of the bed. As she stood, she stepped on one of the down pillows that was half under the bed. Shifting, she stooped to pick it up, knowing she must have pushed it off during the night.

She tossed the pillow onto the bed, then crossed to the windows and tugged back the heavy drapes. A dull gray light came through the heavy leaded windowpanes, with light rain running down the glass. Mallory could make out a world of swirling fog and mist with hints of darkness beyond, all under a sky that looked heavy enough to press down on the world. It was daytime, but there was no sun to tell if it was morning or afternoon. She tugged the drapes back all the way, letting in the dull light, then turned as she raked her hair back from her face.

She stretched her arms over her head, then shivered at the chill. She didn't know what Saxon expected her to do to fill her time here, except that he wanted to have lunch with her to find out what was going on.

And she had plenty to tell him. If he'd wanted to throw his family into turmoil, he'd succeeded.

Mallory walked to the armoire, taking out a pair of her jeans, an oversize white cable sweater and her old running shoes. Once she'd dressed, she'd go and find Saxon. She went into the bathroom, placed her clothes on the vanity, then stripped off her T-shirt. When she turned on the faucet, she was thankful to see the water come out steaming.

Ten minutes later, toweled dry and dressed, she stepped out into the hall and almost ran directly into someone right in front of her door. But this time it wasn't Tony. As she looked up, she found herself facing a stocky man with bright red hair that shagged around a florid face. He wore dark blue work clothes with heavy black boots, and he was staring at the floor.

"Sorry," he muttered as he pushed his hands into the pockets of his soiled jeans and hunched his shoulders forward. Mallory caught a hint of alcohol on his breath as he exhaled. "Myra sent me to get your fire going."

"Oh, good," Mallory said, realizing that her voice sounded slightly raspy and a certain rawness lingered in her throat. "It's freezing in there."

He finally looked up at her with pale blue eyes. "You're the mister's kid?"

"I'm Mallory King."

"Damn the old man," he muttered, and she flinched at the sudden hatred she saw in his eyes. "Damn you, too."

# CHAPTER SEVEN

The man pushed past Mallory, bumping her in the shoulder with his elbow as he headed into her room. She rubbed her shoulder as she turned and saw him head for the stove.

"Close the door and the room'll heat up faster," he said without turning to look at her. He opened the grated door and reached for the poker.

Mallory was glad to leave and shut the door behind her. As she turned to go to Saxon's room, she saw Lawrence in the hallway, leaning against the wall. He looked as if he'd had a rough night. Dark circles under his eyes and the hint of a beard at his jaw were a far cry from the perfectly turned-out man she'd met the night before. He looked as if he was still wearing the clothes he'd had on at dinner, and he had a definite air of dissipation about him.

"So, you met William," he said, the odor of alcohol even stronger than it had been with the other man. "Charming, isn't he?"

"That's William?"

"Yeah, Myra's son. He's as strong as an ox and twice as stupid. Hell, he's thirty years old and Myra still treats him as if he was a kid. But I guess she has her reasons."

The image of Myra as a mother seemed oddly jarring for Mallory. "What reasons?"

"He's given her trouble most of his life. Oh, he's good for the menial labor around this place, but don't cross him."

She remembered the look of hate in his eyes just before he'd gone into the bedroom. "Why not?"

"He's crazy. He gets out of control."

"But Saxon keeps him around?"

"Saxon lets anyone who interests him hang around here. It's sort of like playing with fire, living on the edge, testing the boundaries."

A paraphrasing of Joyce's explanation for Tony being a partner of Saxon's. "It's his house."

"Sure, and William's been here as long as I can remember. Except when he was in jail."

"What was he in jail for?"

"I never got the straight story from Saxon. Myra just sort of ignores the whole thing as if it never happened."

"As if what never happened?"

Lawrence stood straight and ran a hand over the stubble on his face. "It seems that dimwit tried to kill a man."

"He killed a man?" Mallory asked.

"*Tried to.* He *tried* to kill a man."

"How?"

"He went down to the city, had too much to drink—something he does from time to time—and he got nasty. Some poor fool ended up with his throat almost crushed. Willy boy tried to strangle him with his bare hands. He got put in jail for assault and something else. When he got out, he was back here as if nothing ever happened."

"Saxon just took him back?"

"Sure. Even though good old Uncle Saxon hasn't got a drop of charity in his veins, he seems to have a blind spot where Myra's concerned."

"What sort of blind spot?"

"Rumor has it she and Uncle got it on a long time ago."

Mallory stared at Lawrence. "You're kidding."

"No. Not hardly."

She heard something thud in her room, and she glanced at the door. William. When she looked back at Lawrence, she saw him shake his head. "Don't even think it. William arrived here with Myra thirty years ago. His father, whoever he is, stayed in Denmark when Myra immigrated to this country. You're the only bastard of Uncle's that's shown up on the doorstep."

She could feel heat in her face and knew that it would be remarkably easy to hate this smug-looking man. "I was brought here, I didn't just show up."

"No, you were invited here to haunt us all," he murmured.

Mallory felt chilled despite the thickness of her wool sweater, and she rubbed at her arms to try and generate a bit of warmth. "Do you really believe this place is haunted?"

He studied her intently. "With you walking around looking like Kate, I think I might." He grimaced. "And, God, you look disgustingly fresh for a ghost."

Mallory caught a whiff of the stale liquor again, and she knew she didn't want to stand here any longer. "I'll see you later," she said as she started around Lawrence to head for Saxon's room.

"What did Joyce say to you last night?"

The question stopped Mallory and she turned. Lawrence was leaning against the wall, his arms crossed on his chest. "How did you know we talked last night?" she asked.

"I saw her coming out of your room, and I know she wasn't in there welcoming you to the family."

"No, she wasn't."

"Then what did she want?"

Mallory shrugged. "To let me know that she was here first."

"And what did you tell her?"

"That I'm here now."

He straightened abruptly and rubbed at his jaw with one finger. "The question is, for how long?"

Mallory braced herself. "For as long as Saxon wants me here."

"Then we don't have a problem. You'll last a week ... tops."

"How do you know?"

"An educated guess." He stood straight and pushed his hands in the pockets of his rumpled jacket. Then he leaned closer to her, bringing the staleness of alcohol with him. "And a week's hardly enough time for him to write you into his damned will."

"I don't care what he does with his will."

"Sure you don't. And I'm here because I love my uncle." He rocked back, thankfully taking the odor with him. "We're all here for the same reason, cousin."

"Which is?"

"Money. Pure and simple. And you know what they say..."

Dislike welled up in her for this man. "What *do* they say, Lawrence?" she muttered.

"To the victor goes the spoils."

"I thought that only applied to war."

"Hey, don't look now, but this *is* war."

"I'll see you later," she said.

"Where are you heading?"

"To see Saxon."

"He's in his room with Tony. They're having a meeting." He glanced at his wristwatch. "They have been for almost an hour. If I were you, I wouldn't disturb them. The king just might get angry and chop off your little head." His eyes were hard and cold. "And that would be an ugly end for someone as beautiful as you are—even uglier than your mother's swan song."

"Why don't you just go and sleep off your binge?" she said impatiently.

"That's the plan," he agreed. "Then I'll be fresh for the next one. Let me know when you're ready to give up and leave this happy little place."

"I've never walked away from a fight in my life." That was the truth. She'd stood her ground over and over again when she had to, and even though this was all playacting, she knew a child of Saxon Mills wouldn't let Lawrence intimidate her. "I'm not going to start now."

"Have it your way," he murmured, then started past her. Without looking back, he called over his shoulder, "But when *your* ghost starts walking these halls, do me a favor and stay clear of me." His words echoed in the hallway as Lawrence disappeared around a corner, heading for the front of the house.

Mallory had had enough. She wanted air, and that meant getting out of this house. She went back into her bedroom where William was crouched in front of the stove, just now striking a match for the fire he'd laid. He didn't give any sign he knew she was back in the room.

Mallory crossed to the armoire, took out her raincoat, which had been dried and hung next to the expensive clothes. As she went back to the door, she slipped on her coat. Saxon had known exactly what had happened with each of the people who had approached her. Every one of them was in this for the long haul, willing to do whatever it took to get what they thought was rightfully theirs. And God help anyone who got in their way.

Mallory hurried out of the room and headed down the hallway to the balcony. At the stairs, she took one look down the corridor that led to Saxon's room, then started down to the foyer. As she stepped onto the marble floor, she looked around and spotted a hallway angling out from the far corner near the library doors.

She crossed to it, stepped into an arched-ceilinged hallway and followed it past tapestry-covered walls and closed doors, until she came to a massive arch fashioned in stone. She moved into a sprawling kitchen with stainless steel and porcelain everywhere against the backdrop of stone walls and multiple panels of French doors that let the weak light of day into the room.

An old kerosene lantern glowed on a slate counter near a walk-in refrigerator. A massive cutting block in the center of the floor held a large tray filled with pastries and rolls. Mallory took a croissant, then went to the nearest multipaned door and opened it.

Cold misty air invaded the room, and Mallory put on the hood of her coat and stepped outside onto a terrace that seemed to stretch all the way along the back of the house until it met with the glass walls of what looked like a solarium. From what Mallory could make out in the gray drizzle that shrouded the land, there were gardens beyond the terrace ahead of her, the skeletal frame of new construction beyond the glass walls of the solarium, and a turret all but lost in the mist.

She looked to the right and saw steps leading down to a cobbled driveway that cut across an expanse of rolling lawns, then disappeared out of sight into huge oak and eucalyptus trees.

She closed the door and headed down to the driveway, nibbling on the roll in her hand. The cobbles leading from the house were slick with drizzle, and as she got to the trees, huge drops of rain fell from the leaves. Mallory ducked her head as she walked farther from the house.

Finishing the croissant, she brushed her hands together and pushed them into her pockets, hunching her shoulders against the cool wind and drizzle. As she passed a dense stand of eucalyptus trees and turned a corner, she caught sight of a stone structure set at the end of the drive where the cobbles swept into a huge circle. It was a ten-foot statue of a rearing horse, the brass mellowed to deep browns and greens, its surface gleaming with rain.

The sprawling building beyond it had a steep slate roof turned deep navy from the rain and there were splashes of color along the gray of the rock wall from low-growing flowers. It spread out in both directions, with massive trees protecting much of it from the storm. As she got closer, Mallory could see spaced archways in the stone walls, with wooden doors that were closed against the elements.

In the center, under the highest peak of the roof, were enormous sliding doors that had been left open to show a hay-storage area. The pungency of composting hay and manure touched the cool air, and she heard the faint whinny of a horse from inside as she went closer. Memories of childhood daydreams about owning a horse came to her, fantasies of having her own white mare and riding her across meadows and along the water's edge at the beach as the surf surged toward the sands.

Daydreams had been the only escape from the dingy rooming houses she'd lived in with her mother, then the succession of foster homes she'd endured. But she'd never actually been closer to a horse than picture books or the single time she'd gone to the circus with her mother. There had been fanciful calliope music, silly clowns that made her laugh, and horses ridden by beautiful women. "Horses are magical, sweetheart," her mother had said. And they had been for her ever since.

She approached the open doors, then stepped through into the protection of the stable. The flat stone floors were partially covered by straw, and hay was stacked high in the middle, leaving wide aisles on either side that went right through the building to another set of open doors.

Mallory went farther into the stables, until she reached an intersecting aisle. She looked to the left at four or five stalls on each side, with wire mesh on top and wood on the bottom. They were empty. When she looked to her right, she saw more stalls along the aisle, but there were horses in two of these. The tops were open, and in the corner stall, a horse, the color of vanilla, with a mane of pure white and an elegant head, was looking at her through the open top.

Directly across the aisle, in the other corner, was a large, raw-boned horse, with rippling muscles under a coat as black as night and a single spot of white set between eyes that looked wild and restless. He threw his head back, snorting and pawing the ground, his ebony mane long and silky, and his nostrils flared.

Mallory went closer to the pale horse, cautiously putting out her hand, and was pleased when the horse nuzzled at her. She felt the heat of its breath on her hand, then the silky warmth of its muzzle against her skin. "Hello there," she said softly, instinctively lowering her voice to reassure the animal. "Atta girl. Atta girl." The horse let her gently stroke the side of its jaw. "You are a girl, aren't you?"

"A mare."

Her hand jerked slightly when Tony spoke behind her, and the horse drew back. Mallory didn't turn. She kept holding out her hand, trying to coax the horse to come back.

"A mare," she repeated softly, her chest tightening with a sudden uneasiness, probably a remnant from the nightmare. "What's her name?"

"Saxon's Folly III."

She could tell he was coming closer as he talked, then she sensed him right behind her. The air seemed to thin, and the nightmare came back with a clarity that shook her. She could almost taste the fear, and she deliberately took a deep breath just to make sure she could still do it.

With that breath, she inhaled a certain maleness that seemed to cling to Tony, and it mingled strangely with a tinge of fear that nudged at her. "I guess the question is, what are number one and number two in the Saxon's Folly department?"

"Saxon never actually told me, but I'd guess number two is this place." He was so close she could feel him brush the sleeve of her coat, and tension tugged at her shoulder and neck. "The never-ending construction and the horrendous upkeep could be classified as folly, I suppose."

"And number one?"

"Your mother... for the obvious reasons."

The horse came closer, letting her stroke the silkiness of its muzzle, which covered an unsteadiness in her hand. If she looked to her right, she would be able to see Tony clearly, so she stared determinedly at the horse. "Why is this horse a folly?"

"She can't run."

Mallory cast him a cautious look, not at all prepared to finally see his image etched in the gray light of morning. His hair was damp from rain, slicked back from his angular, clean-shaven face. His skin tone was darker than she remembered, and the impact of his gaze meeting hers was undiminished by the touch of shadows from the poor light. In an open beige jacket darkened by rain at the shoulders, a turtlenecked black shirt and tight jeans, he looked diametrically different from the man in the suit last night.

But his impact on her wasn't changed. The man was almost uncomfortably male, and each encounter left her more and more uneasy on many levels.

"Is she lame or something?" she asked, although the horse looked perfect to her.

"No. She just doesn't have a killer instinct. That's the big thing in any race, having the heart to kill or be killed." When he reached out to touch the horse, he brushed Mallory's hand, and she drew back quickly. The last thing she wanted was to have physical contact with this man. He cast her a slanting look. "How about you?"

She looked away from him, but found her gaze falling on his hand stroking the horse's neck. Strong fingers, a strong hand, square nails and no jewelry. She quickly looked away, feigning casual interest in the structure of the stables. "What about me?"

"Do you have a killer's instinct, the heart to go for broke and damn the consequences?"

She stared hard at the black horse in the stall on the opposite side of the aisle, keeping her shoulder turned away from Tony. "I don't know."

"You're in the middle of a family that does."

"Does that include you?"

He exhaled sharply. "Especially me. I was weaned on it, and it's something that just sort of stays with you. Maybe a defective gene pool. I don't know. But it's there."

She heard a tinge of distaste in his tone and turned to look back at the horse. She'd shifted to start munching on fresh alfalfa in her feeding bin. "So what do you do to the horses that don't have it?"

"Shoot them."

The blunt words ran riot over her already-frayed nerves, and she jerked around to look at Tony. He stood by the stall door, not more than two feet from her, his hands pushed into the pockets of his jeans, his dark eyes on her.

"They wouldn't—"

"No, not Fancy. She's good for pleasure riding. As long as she has something to give Saxon, he'll keep her. When that stops, he'll get rid of her, one way or another."

Rain struck the roof and pavement outside the stables, and the breeze pushed cold air through the open center. Mallory shivered and hugged her arms around herself. "Just like that?"

"Just like that." He shook his head. "And he'd do that to you. I wasn't kidding about that."

She turned from Tony to walk into the central area and toward the open back doors. She stared out at rain that had grown from a mist to a steady downpour. Grayness seemed to be everywhere, color a thing of memory only, just the way her life in San Francisco was beginning to feel. She rubbed at her arms with the flats of her hands to generate some warmth. "What makes you such an authority on my father?"

She heard him shift, the scuff of loose hay under his shoes, then she could literally sense his closeness. But he didn't touch her. She knew he was at her side, looking out at a rain-soaked oak tree set in the middle of muddy paddocks and the vineyards beyond. "I had a father much like Saxon. That's probably why I can deal with him, and why I don't have any illusions about his sort of man."

A man connected with the mob wasn't exactly like Saxon, she thought. "What sort is that?"

"A driven man, a man who is probably empty inside, so he tries to control as much of this world as he can."

"Joseph Danforth."

She heard him take a sharp breath. "So, Joyce has been talking about me, hasn't she? I should have expected it."

"It's true what she said about your father?"

"My father?" he said in a low voice. "I don't have one."

She glanced at him, thankfully finding him watching the rain outside. His profile was set and hard looking, his jaw held tight. She noticed for the first time that he had a faint scar just under his ear. The faint line cut jaggedly down the side of his throat and disappeared into the collar of his jacket.

"Joyce said—"

He turned to pin her with his dark gaze, and she was shocked to see an edge of pain in his eyes. "I can imagine what Joyce said. The truth is my father's dead. He died in prison."

She stared at him; pain that didn't touch his cold words was evident in his eyes. "I'm sorry. I—"

"Don't be. He died two years ago, but he was gone for me long before that."

"Your last name...Carella?"

"I might have been born Danforth, but there was a point when I didn't want to answer to it anymore. I legally took my mother's maiden name."

"What about your mother?"

His eyes narrowed to help contain the pain that lingered there. "She died almost ten years ago, thankfully before my father was arrested, and I changed my name five years before his house of cards collapsed."

"You just turned your back on him?"

"That's why I'm telling you to get the hell out of here. You don't need this. No amount of money is worth what you're inheriting here."

"Maybe I could make things better."

Her words brought a shake of his head. "If I thought you meant that, I'd laugh."

"I do mean it," she said, knowing if this was all true, if Saxon really *were* her father, she'd stay and do whatever it took to make it work.

"Then you're a fool."

"Thanks," she muttered, turning away from him.

"Take my offer," he said softly, so close that she could swear she felt the heat of his breath on her neck.

She stood very still, not daring to move, not when every atom of her body seemed to be on fire from the man's closeness. "No."

"Reconsider."

"No."

"I'll go higher."

She spun around, shocked that he was still where she'd left him. He hadn't moved closer, after all. She had only imagined that he was right next to her. "No."

Now he did take a step to diminish the distance between them, and it took all her willpower to stand her ground. "Two hundred thousand, and you're free of all this. No ties, no obligations, no burden so heavy you'll wish you were dead or wish your father was dead."

"No," she whispered, her fingers digging into her upper arms.

"Name your price."

"I told you last night that you don't have enough money."

His expression darkened. "Then you do have a price."

"I don't. I wouldn't turn my back on my family just because they didn't turn out to be Ozzie and Harriet."

He reached out without warning and cupped her chin with his fingers. His heat seemed to brand her, and she stood very still. "This so-called family of yours gives new meaning to the word *dysfunctional*."

"But they're my family," she whispered unsteadily.

"Are you that desperate for a family?"

Oh, God, if he only knew how desperate she'd been all her life to have a family. She closed her eyes and swallowed hard, then looked at him. "You don't get to pick and choose family. Not everyone can just turn their backs and walk away."

His hold on her hovered just this side of pain. "You think it was easy for me?"

Suddenly the heavens were shattered by bright light as lightning tore through the grayness, and an explosion rocked the world. Mallory spun out of Tony's hold and saw the oak tree rip apart, the power of the lightning cutting it in half and exploding flames in its heart.

It was like a nightmare, with flames rising into rain, and smoke swirling with mists and wind. Mallory was consumed by a fear she had never known before, and she turned, ready to run, but Tony was there. He reached out to her, and she fell into his arms, into heat and safety.

And she felt as if she were reliving the dream, when Tony held her and he was her anchor, her salvation. But when she lifted her head, it wasn't fear that she felt. His hand touched her face, his thumb moving slowly on her cool skin, then brushing across her bottom lip as lightly as a feather.

An echo of the nightmare, but now his hand wasn't pressed to her mouth. His thumb again traced the line of her lip, and his touch shot fire, not fear, through her. "Nothing's easy in this world," he whispered, and his voice trailed off as his thumb rested on her chin.

"I know."

He was motionless for a long moment, then slowly, ever so slowly, he leaned toward her. The touch of his lips on hers was shockingly warm and tender. The contact was an exploration, not a demand, and it held none of the chill that surrounded them.

His hands framed her face, and he slanted his mouth over hers. Without needing to think, she parted her lips, welcoming his exploration, and when his tongue traced her teeth, then invaded her mouth, she leaned toward him. She felt his body against hers, the strength of desire drawing her closer and closer to him.

Her arms circled his neck, and she held on to him, stunned by the passion that came to her in a burst of white-hot fire. Nothing like it had ever happened to her before. Nothing this stunning and all-consuming. Kisses had been kisses for her, never something that seemed to drain the soul from her. They'd been tentative, searching, never searing and almost frightening in their intensity.

Yet that fear just egged her need on, giving it a sensual edge that took her breath away. Brilliance flashed around her and through her as lightning struck again, and everything seemed to vibrate deeply. She was lost in something that defied description and denied every rational action in her life before coming to this house.

This was a role, an unscripted play, and she was the center of it. The daughter who wasn't, who didn't exist. The family that never could be. And this man, the lover who could rob her of sanity and fill her with desire. His tongue invaded her heat, and his hands skimmed lower, over her shoulders, dipping to the small of her back to pull her securely against him.

He wanted her; there was no hiding it. But the world began to teeter horribly when Mallory knew he wanted Saxon Mills's daughter, the heir to the Mills fortune.

As that thought fell unflinchingly into place, Mallory felt as if she'd died. Tony wasn't here for her. He wasn't comforting her. He wasn't shielding her from the devastation that had destroyed the tree. He wasn't pressing his body against hers, or becoming aroused by her.

He didn't want Mallory King. She knew what he wanted, and there was no way she could give it to him. What he wanted didn't exist. Not any more than this moment in time could keep happening. It was a fantasy as much as her place in this family was. And the fantasy had to end right here.

# CHAPTER EIGHT

Tony could feel Mallory freeze. One moment she was against him, holding on to him, moving in a way that drew fire from him, and the next she was motionless. Even before she eased back from him, he knew whatever had happened between them was gone. When he felt her hands slip from him, and her body leave contact with his, he didn't have to look at her to realize that mistakes in his life just seemed to pile up around him.

He met the stunned look in her deep blue eyes, and he had to steel himself not to reach out to her again. He had to keep the distance between them intact. "That was a mistake," she breathed in an unsteady voice. "I'm sorry."

"I'm not," he said truthfully. All he regretted was the sudden change in her.

She turned from him to stare at the shattered oak that was still smoldering. She bit her bottom lip until it was almost bloodless, then he heard her take a shaky breath. "I was startled by the lightning, and I reacted without thinking. It was an impulse, and it was a mistake."

He couldn't take his eyes off Mallory. The sweep of her throat, as she raised her chin slightly as if daring him to argue, only made him think of tasting her. The dark curls that had loosened from her hair clip made him ache to touch her, and the taste of her, still on his lips, taunted him.

When he'd touched her, it hadn't mattered who she was, who her father was or what hold she had over everyone at this place. All that mattered was silky skin, heat, enormous blue eyes and the fragrance that clung to her and made him think of sunlight even in this storm.

When another flash of lightning ripped through the skies, bathing her in a white light that only succeeded in defining everything right about her, he muttered, "Impulses can be dangerous things." He deliberately pushed his hands behind his back to kill his own impulses, and he looked out at the storm that was building in force again.

"You don't even know me," she said softly.

He looked back at her, unsettled by how vulnerable she looked in that moment. "I know that you shouldn't be here."

Before she could say anything, the sound of an oath made her jump. Tony turned to see William running down the aisle toward them. His yellow rain slicker flapped around him, striking his black rubber boots, and rain ran off the brim of his hat.

"Did you see that?" he asked as he came to a stop right between Tony and Mallory and looked out at the smoldering oak. "Damn. It sounded like dynamite, didn't it?" He turned to glance at Mallory. "Hey, the mister's expecting you soon."

"What time is it?"

"Eleven-thirty."

"Thanks," she murmured, then flipped up the hood of her jacket and headed for the front of the stable.

Tony could almost feel her relief at having an excuse to leave him, and it left a bad taste in his mouth. He kept his eyes on her until she ducked out into the rain and took off at a jog toward the house.

Tony turned and looked at William. "How about the generator? Is it fixed yet?"

The man shook his head as he snatched off his rain cap and slapped it against the side of his coat. "You don't see no lights on out here, do you? It's all froze up from not being used. Looks like we're out of luck until this storm's over and they get the power poles fixed."

"Any idea how long that's going to be?"

He narrowed his eyes on Tony. "A day or a week. Who knows? Until then, we're cut off and out of luck. Speaking of luck, yours is gonna run out if you mess with the mister's daughter."

Tony stared at William. "What does that mean?"

He shrugged. "Don't have to be a mind reader to know you'd crawl into bed with her if you could."

That was all too close to the truth for Tony, and he wanted to stop the images the man's words were conjuring up in an imagination that didn't need much help when it came to the idea of making love to Mallory. "You son of a—"

William grinned suggestively at him. "Hey, you were all over her."

"You were watching us?"

"Yeah, but I didn't want to break in, though. So I waited." The smirk on his face was enough for Tony to know the man probably would have watched if he and Mallory had made love in the hay, and it made his skin crawl. "You know, if the mister knew about this, he would toss your butt out of here and cut you off."

Tony's nerves were already raw from his encounter with Mallory, and this man only fueled an anger that felt like fire in his belly. He stopped the man's words by reaching out and gripping his shoulder. When he pressed his fingers into the slick rubber of the man's raincoat, he felt William tense.

Tony knew that even though William was a big man, he was a coward unless he was drunk. "If Saxon knew about other things, he'd cut a lot of people off at the pass, wouldn't he?" He stared hard at William. "And we don't want him to do that, do we?"

William's eyes dropped. "Whatever."

"Do we understand each other, William?"

"Yeah, I guess so." He looked up at Tony. "You do whatever you want with her. She's not going anywhere."

"What does that mean?"

"Her car's still where it got stuck." He shrugged out of Tony's hold. "The mister told me to leave it there, to get her stuff out of it, but don't try to get it out until he said for me to."

Saxon never let his control slip, even taking away any choice Mallory had about leaving before the storm let up. "You did what you were told?"

"Always do," he muttered, then turned and headed into the side wing of the stable. "Gotta get something to take care of that tree."

Tony stood alone in the stables, the fury of the storm crashing all around, and he had a sensation of loneliness that was staggering. He never thought much about being alone. He had chosen that when he walked away from his family and everything it entailed. But from the moment Mallory walked out of the stable and disappeared into the storm, he knew he was really alone.

He remembered the feel of her in his arms, and the taste of her on his lips, and his body responded instantly. "Damn it all," he muttered, and as he turned to leave, something glinted in the hay by his feet.

He crouched down and saw Mallory's clip. He picked it up, then closed his hand over the smooth silver and stood. Pushing his hands in his pockets, he crossed to the open doors, then, without hesitating, plunged out into the storm. He almost welcomed the cold rain that stung his face and soaked his clothes. But nothing could really put out the fire that burned in him.

By the time Mallory approached the door to Saxon's suite at ten minutes past twelve, she was dry and relatively calm, and had changed into fresh jeans and a blue buttoned sweater. Tony's kiss had shocked her, almost as much as her reaction to it. But she'd stopped it before it went too far, and she had to leave it at that.

Her past relationships had been fleeting and basically unsatisfactory. And she'd always moved on before she got too close to anyone. But the moment she'd let Tony kiss her, she'd realized how devastating that caress could be. A kiss was not just a kiss. It was as powerful as anything she'd experienced in her life, and it scared her.

She knocked on the door, and when there was no sound from inside, she pressed the latch and opened the barrier. As she cautiously stepped inside, she saw fire crackling in the hearth, and the drapes tightly closed against the storm outside. She had that sense of being watched and turned to her right.

Saxon was staring at her from where he stood by a side door, but he didn't say a thing.

"Saxon?" she finally said.

His eyes narrowed. "You finally came," he said softly.

"I'm sorry I'm late, but I couldn't get my hair to dry," she said, turning to swing the door shut. When she turned back again, Saxon had crossed the room and was standing by the hearth.

He held his hands palms out to the warmth of the blaze. "I wondered if you were going to come at all."

She didn't understand why he'd think she wouldn't come. "Of course I was. You asked me to. Besides, we need to talk."

He cast her a slanting glance. "Where were you?"

"In the stables."

Mallory watched him as he turned to stare into the dancing flames. His navy shirt and dark slacks set off the whiteness of his hair and the wiry leanness of his body. Despite his years, he held himself well, with a sense of pride, and for a second she thought she could almost catch a glimpse of the man he must have been when he'd known Kate. Tall and square-shouldered, with an almost regal bearing, rich...and manipulative.

He wasn't a man a person could feel comfortable around, and she was glad she wouldn't be here beyond two weeks. She didn't know if she could take the tension he produced in her any more than she could take the tension Tony seemed intent on building in her.

"You can't leave, you know," he said without warning as he rubbed his hands together by the heat. "The storm's cut us off completely. Even the electricity."

She stared at his back. "I know. But I don't think it'll last more than a couple of days."

"There are mud slides down the way, so there's no way to get past until they're cleared."

"When the rain's stopped, maybe there'll be a way around."

His hands stilled. "Why are you so anxious to leave?" he demanded in a low voice.

This didn't make sense. "Excuse me?"

He turned, his deep blue eyes wider than normal. "I don't want you to leave."

"We agreed—"

Suddenly he moved toward her, but stopped two feet from her. "We agreed? You make this all sound like some business deal."

"Saxon, that's exactly—"

She could see real anger burning in his eyes, and an unsteadiness in his hands as he held them at his side. "You can't do this for love? You can't stay because I want you to?"

She blinked, shocked by his tone and words. He'd said they could talk freely in here. They didn't have to keep up pretenses. But he was talking as if he was still playing the part, and she was really someone close to him, someone he wanted to keep forever. She could almost believe he thought she was Kate. She didn't understand any of this, but decided to go along with it.

"Of course, I'll stay," she said.

He reached out and touched her cheek, his fingers chilly despite the time he'd spent in front of the fire. "I knew you would. I knew it."

And she knew he wasn't playing a part. He was living it. "I want to stay," she said as calmly as she could, wondering if she could make it to the door before he could reach her. "I promise."

His hand was still on her, and she felt it tremble against her cheek. "You promise?"

"Yes, I do," she whispered. "Saxon?"

He didn't respond.

"Saxon," she repeated softly. "I'm Mallory. Mallory."

His eyes fluttered, then his hand slowly drew back and he nodded. "Yes, Mallory. Of course." He ran one hand over his face and murmured, "Of course."

She watched him cautiously. "Are you all right?"

He turned and crossed to the chairs and table near the fireplace. "Yes, I'm…I'm just…" He sank down in one of the chairs and clasped his hands in his lap. He suddenly looked older than he had just moments ago. "I'm just a bit tired. I've been working hard on..." His voice trailed off as he turned and looked at her.

"Come and sit." He flicked a hand in her direction. "Myra brought us lunch. It might still be warm."

She would have left then, but for some reason she felt a degree of compassion for this man. He might have the business world and his family on their knees, but he was still human and obviously isolated in a way that Mallory could only guess at.

She took the seat she'd used when they'd had their first meeting, and watched Saxon reach forward to take the domed cover off a tray on the table. "Chicken, just the way I like it," he murmured as he put the lid off to one side. Then he looked at Mallory and motioned to the two artistically arranged plates of broiled chicken, green salad and steamed vegetables. "Please, eat."

She ignored the food for a moment. "Saxon, I don't understand what that was all about."

A degree of respect for the man surfaced when he didn't try to pretend he didn't know what she was talking about. He sank back in the chair and met her gaze directly. "I'm sorry about that. I was thinking of Kate, and when you came in with your hair all up... For a moment, just a moment, in this light, you looked so like her. I don't think I was really prepared for your real likeness to her." It obviously didn't give him much pleasure. There was a tinge of anger still in his expression.

"Maybe I shouldn't wear my hair up again."

"No, wear it like that," he said, his expression tight, emphasizing deep lines at his mouth and between his eyes. "Let the others know what it is for Kate to haunt them, too."

Mallory watched him as he spoke, the idea that he was quite mad not so farfetched. "If you're trying to forget her, this is a very strange way for you to do it."

The shadow of a smile flitted over his face. "Who said I wanted to forget?"

"I just thought—"

"I told you, don't assume anything." He sat forward and reached for a napkin by his plate. "Just do what I ask you to do."

"Of course," she murmured.

He shook out his napkin and, after placing it in his lap, moved closer and picked up a roll. "Enough of this. Tell me, how do you think it went last night?"

She sat very still, any appetite she might have had, gone. "If you wanted to stir up a hornet's nest, I'd say you did it. Everyone's in a tizzy, and every one of them wants me out of here . . . one way or another."

Mallory watched him tear the roll in half and take his time spreading it with butter from a tiny crockery dish before he finally looked back to her. "They're all so predictable," he murmured. "So predictable."

"And you knew what was going to happen."

"Or course. Lawrence probably got drunk and tried to talk you out of staying. Joyce would try and wave her pedigree in front of you and shame you. Myra will make you feel as uncomfortable as she can. And Tony, he'll try to buy you off. He's probably not above using force like his father would have."

The flashing memory of the nightmare overlapped with the kiss in the stables, and Mallory had to force herself not to rub at her lips. "You're right about all of them," she said, deliberately avoiding further discussion of Tony.

"I thought so."

"What about William?"

His hands stilled. "What about him?"

"Why would he hate me...or at least someone he thinks is your daughter?"

He laid the roll on his plate untouched and sat back. His eyes were hooded and unreadable. "William is different. I don't want you having anything to do with him beyond his duties in the household."

"Why?"

He waved that aside with a flick of his hand. "Just do it."

He was imperious, Mallory thought, but she didn't ask any more questions about William or Tony. Instead, she nibbled at her lunch without enthusiasm, and the only sounds in the room were of the storm outside and the crackle of the fire in the hearth.

When Saxon pushed back his cleared plate and dropped the napkin on it, he said, "Isn't there anything you want to discuss with me?"

Thankful to give up the pretext of eating, she duplicated his actions, then sat back in her chair. "What am I supposed to do to fill the time during these two weeks?"

"Check out the house. That will take you a long time, and then there's the grounds and the vineyard. When the storm lets up, go riding around the property." He glanced right at her. "You said you were in the stables earlier. You know where they are, and the facilities are yours to use.''

"I'd love to, but I've never really ridden.''

"Then learn to ride. You can use Folly. She's easy enough in her gait and disposition.''

"Tony said she doesn't have the instincts to race.''

He frowned. "Why would Tony tell you that?''

"It's not true?''

"Oh, it's true. I was just wondering when Tony would have said that?''

"Earlier today.''

His frown deepened. "Folly's cost me a great deal. I went by her bloodlines, and they were exceptional. She turned out to be a throwback to a rather pacifistic relative somewhere in her past.'' He shook his head. "I think that's how Tony likes to see himself, as the pacifist in a lineage of blood-thirsty cutthroats.''

"Is he?''

"A pacifist?''

"Yes.''

"He likes to think he is, but no, he's not. He goes for the throat. He just couches his barbarianism in civil actions and boardroom tactics.'' He reached for the goblet of wine and took a sip. "Did Tony tell you about his father?''

"A bit. I don't think he likes to talk about it too much.''

"I never understood that. His father was very effective until he got betrayed by a partner who was trying to buy himself a deal with the government.'' He lifted an eyebrow questioningly. "You've heard of Joseph Danforth, haven't you?''

"Who hasn't?"

"They caught him on tax evasion, but they would have loved to get him on extortion, or fraud, or—God knows—maybe even murder."

Mallory cringed at his words. "You don't mean that, do you?"

"Of course I do."

She remembered the tenderness in Tony's touch just before he kissed her. "But, Tony—"

"Is Joseph Danforth's son, his blood kin. He might change his name, and he might wear three-piece suits, and he might go to litigation rather than putting a contract out on someone, but he's got as black a heart as his father ever had." Saxon rubbed his hands together. "That's why he's so good at business."

"If he's that good, why don't you give him what he wants and put him in control of the businesses when you have to make a decision about it?"

Saxon looked genuinely taken aback by what she thought was a logical question. "Why would I? He's not my blood."

"So it's really between Joyce and Lawrence?"

He dropped his fork on his plate with a sharp clatter. "I won't leave a penny or a share of stock to anyone who isn't from my bloodline. It's that simple. And if I had anyone besides Joyce and Lawrence, I wouldn't hesitate giving it to them. But not to Tony."

"Then why's Tony here at all?"

"Because he has shares equal to mine in all our business dealings, and he thinks he can talk me into giving him control of mine."

"Why don't you tell him he doesn't stand a chance?"

"I don't want to drive him off. Whoever takes over my business affairs will need Tony's help. I'll explain that to him when I'm damn good and ready to do it."

Mallory felt bitterness burn at the back of her throat. "You'll use him, trap him into a situation he can't afford to walk away from, then tell him he's getting nothing he thinks he's going to get. That's hardly fair."

His sudden burst of laughter sounded rough and sharp, and as jarring as anything Mallory had ever heard. As it died off, she watched Saxon swipe at his eyes. "God, that's funny. I haven't laughed that hard in a very long time."

Mallory glared at him, then stood and crossed to the hearth where the fire was beginning to burn itself out. "Why would you do that to someone you supposedly respect in your business dealings?"

"He offered you money to get out, didn't he?"

"Yes."

"Perfect, perfect," he murmured behind her. "How much?"

"Two hundred thousand dollars."

"What did you tell him?"

"That he didn't have enough money to buy me off."

"Bravo," he murmured, and as she turned, he lifted his hands toward her and affected a mock clapping. "A great comeback. But it's a shame."

"What is?"

He raised one eyebrow. "You should have taken it."

She thought the man couldn't surprise her again, but he had. "I couldn't. I mean, that's ridiculous."

The fire touched his eyes with a strange glow and for a moment she thought she was looking into the face of madness. "It's not ridiculous. If he offers it again, take it."

"And leave?"

"No, of course not. You don't have to do what he wants you to do. Just take it and smile. What's he going to do—go to the police? Besides, he'd do anything to get what he wants. Money's just his first option. Take advantage of it."

Mallory remembered the kiss and knew that romancing her was probably another option. Her stomach knotted. "I wouldn't do that for money," she whispered.

"Why? You're not above lying as long as the money's right. Look what you're doing for me. And I'm paying you a hell of a lot less than Tony's willing to pay."

"This is a job, a role." The heat of the fire at her back was making the chill in front of her even more pronounced.

"You're right. You're pretending. If you were a real Mills, you'd have taken the money and laughed in his face."

She almost said, *Thank goodness I'm not,* but instead she murmured, "Bloodlines."

"Exactly." Saxon stood abruptly. "Now I'm tired." She was dismissed and she was thankful to make her escape. But as she turned to leave, Saxon stopped her. "One more thing."

She glanced at him standing by his chair, his hand gripping the back. "Yes?"

"We will have lunch together every day except on Christmas and New Year's."

She'd almost forgotten about the holidays. And she'd thought Saxon would, too. She thought his celebration would be a "Bah, humbug" and nothing much else. The house wasn't exactly abounding with the spirit of the season, despite the decorations laid out with precision in the foyer and dining hall. "What about those days?"

"We will have the family meal at midday. On Christmas, we exchange presents on Christmas Eve."

"Presents?"

"Don't worry. I have that covered. Tonight dinner will be served at seven. Wear the white."

That reminded her. She reached in her pocket and took out the sapphire pendant. "Here," she said, holding it out to Saxon. "I almost forgot."

He looked at the jewelry in her hand, then slowly took it from her. "It's quite lovely, isn't it?" he asked as he held it up by its delicate chain and let it rotate slowly in front of him.

"Was it really Kate's?" Mallory asked.

He stared at it hard. "Until she threw it back at me."

"It's beautiful," Mallory said.

"I should sell it or give it away," he muttered, letting it fall to the table. It landed with a clatter on the metal tray, just missing the butter crock. He looked at Mallory. "I'll see you just before seven."

She nodded and walked to the door. As she gripped the latch and pulled it open, Saxon spoke again. "Mallory, one more rule you might be aware of is that you keep nothing from me."

She turned to find him still by the table, and she could see the faint glitter of the pendant still on the tray. "I'm not keeping anything from you."

He seemed to tense from the inside out. "I hate liars," he rasped.

"Saxon, I've never lied to you," she said, thankful the door was open and she could make an escape if he started into one of his delusions again.

"Lying by omission is fine with you, is that it?"

The changes in the man rocked Mallory, leaving her feeling as if she were dealing with someone other than the man she'd had lunch with. "Lying by omission, Saxon?"

"Kate did that, neatly slipping past the truth when it suited her purposes."

"I'm not Kate, Saxon," she said with as much calmness as she could muster.

"Then why haven't you told me about what happened at the stables when you were down there with Tony?"

# CHAPTER NINE

Mallory didn't have to look more closely at his eyes to know Saxon knew about her encounter with Tony. Somehow he knew, but she forced a bluff. "What are you talking about?"

He came toward her, and she tightened her hold on the door latch. Two steps, and she could be out in the hall. And after that, she'd be out the door, storm or no storm.

"You were at the stables, you admitted to that."

"Of course, I told you I was."

"You weren't alone." His eyes narrowed, becoming almost predatory. "Tony was there."

She thought of telling him the unvarnished truth, but something stopped her. If he had her confused with Kate, if the reason Kate ran from him years ago was jealousy, if she admitted to kissing Tony, she didn't know what Saxon would do. She couldn't take that chance.

"We were both trying to stay dry and out of the storm."

"And what happened while you were there trying to stay dry with Tony?"

"Why don't you ask *me*, Saxon?"

Mallory spun around and found Tony standing in the hall behind her. In a silky white shirt with full sleeves and buttoned to the neck, worn with snug black slacks, he looked striking, a man formed of lights and darks.

His hair was combed straight back from his face, and his deep brown eyes were partially shadowed by the low light, but she could tell he was staring past her at Saxon.

"I was talking to my daughter. Why are you here?"

"We had an appointment," Tony murmured, casting Mallory a quick glance that had the impact of sudden lightning on her. When he strode past her and into the room, his scent assailed her senses. Tony glanced at his wristwatch. "It's one-fifteen." He looked right at Saxon. "I know how you demand punctuality."

The old man turned and went back to his chair, silently sinking down in the leather once again. He looked at Mallory near the door, but spoke to Tony. "Yes, I do."

"Good. We've got a lot of things to talk about, he said calmly. "But before we settle down to business, why don't you tell me what you were asking Mallory?"

The steady beating of rain on the windows was the only sound for a long moment. Then Saxon looked at Tony. "Mallory said you were in the stables with her earlier."

Tony tucked the tips of his fingers in the pockets of his slacks and shrugged. "Yes, we were. We saw the old oak on the back side of the stables take a direct lightning hit."

Saxon frowned. "William told me about it."

Mallory knew that was how Saxon knew about her time with Tony. "It split and burned. I'd bet it's still smoldering, despite the rain."

Saxon stood abruptly and, with a shocking change of attitude, he looked past Tony and smiled at Mallory. "Dinner's at seven. I'll come to your room to escort you down."

Mallory didn't trust herself to speak. She nodded and turned, pulling the door shut behind her. As she hurried toward her room, she felt such relief to be away from both men that she was almost heady with it. She crossed the balcony, hurried down the hallway, then quickly opened her door. When she went inside, she locked it behind her.

The room was darkened by curtains pulled across the windows, lit only by candles on the table and both nightstands. The scent of woodsmoke touched the warm air, and the stove glowed with heat. The bed had been made, the pillows put back in place and the damp clothes she'd spread on the chair by the stove were gone.

Mallory relished the sense of being alone, but only for a moment. As she moved into the room, she could feel she was being watched. It made the hairs at the back of her neck prickle and she knew she wasn't going to stay in here. She went back out into the hallway and walked toward the stairs.

Something had been eating at her since she came to the house. She hadn't seen a telephone that she could remember, and she wanted to call the city to find out how Sara was doing. As she headed down the stairs, she realized it seemed like an eternity since the accident had happened. And the memory of the accident put things in perspective. What was a houseful of irrational people compared to almost being killed in the rain outside the theater?

She stepped into the foyer, trying to block the memory of Sara crumpled on the street like a soggy doll with rain running around her in rivers. The umbrella had been in the gutter, crushed and twisted. *Her* umbrella. It could have been her crossing that street.

She went back down the hallway into the kitchen. It was empty, but she saw a phone sitting on a stone shelf by a series of open cabinets on the far wall. She crossed and picked it up, but there was no dial tone. She jiggled the disconnect buttons, but nothing happened. The phones were out, too.

She turned and was about to leave the room when she saw the tray that had been in Saxon's suite. Myra must have come for it immediately after she left, and it surprised her that she hadn't seen the woman in the hallway. When she went closer, she saw the napkins laid over the dirty dishes, and peeking out from under the hem of one napkin was the necklace.

She moved the napkin and picked up the pendant, then closed her hand around it. She'd take it back to her room and give it to Saxon later, when he was more rational. If she left it here, goodness knew where it would end up. She looked around, then went to the back doors and peered out at the rain. As she glanced to her left, she saw the solarium and the shadow of the construction beyond it.

She turned and spotted a door across the room. Before she went back up to her own room, she'd work off some of the nervous energy she had by exploring this house. She approached the door, opened it and stepped into a breakfast room filled with plants and wicker furniture. As lightning lit up the windows, Mallory went across the room and through an open arch into the formal dining room.

By the time she went up the stairs to her room, she'd gone through the house and into a wing that she hadn't even known was there. She found flowers that looked like summer in the solarium, and several sitting rooms that appeared to be seldom used. Some of the rooms were closed off, their furnishings covered with dust clothes, and the new wing that Saxon was having built had smelled of plaster and paint.

She got to her door and reached for the latch, but she stopped when the door swung open with a low squeaking sound. Hesitantly, she nudged the door all the way back so she could see into the room before she went inside. Everything looked the same until she caught sight of the area by the stove and table.

A tray sat in the middle of the table and on it were several goblets and a carafe that looked as if it were filled with red wine. But the room was empty. She went inside, threw the bolt and leaned back against the door. She realized that every time she stepped into this room, she was testing it, to see if she felt alone or if something or someone was there with her.

As she leaned back against the door, she couldn't sense anything but the faint chill as the fire in the stove went down. Relieved, she was about to go to the table when someone knocked on her door, making the wood vibrate against her back. She stood very still, but the knocking came again, soft but insistent.

Finally, she turned and opened the door. When she saw Tony in the hallway, her impulse to just shut the door on him had barely formed before he moved closer, making it impossible to close the wooden barrier. He held one finger to his lips and shook his head.

"What do you—?"

Before she understood what was happening, he lunged at her, circling her waist with one hand to pull her against him. The crazy idea he was going to kiss her again was gone in a heartbeat when he pressed his other hand over her mouth. It was like the dream, the terror of being overwhelmed, of having her air cut off.

Mallory tried to scream against his hand, but the sounds were muffled and weak, and her strength was no match for his. He controlled her with an ease that was terrifying, pinning her against his hard strength. As he literally lifted her off her feet, she kicked out and knew the satisfaction of feeling her shoe impact with his shin.

The next instant, he had her inside her room, and he kicked the door shut after them as he carried her farther inside. Then she was free, stumbling backward until she felt the bedpost strike her in the back. As she gasped for air, she tried to think of what to do, but Tony didn't come toward her. He stayed where he was in the middle of the room, seemingly unfazed by the kick to the shin.

He held up his hands, palms out toward her. "I didn't mean to scare you," he said in a low voice.

"What did you think you were doing?" she gasped.

"Keep your voice down. I'm sorry about all this, but we need to talk."

"You could have just asked," she muttered as she rubbed at her mouth where he'd held her.

He glanced over his shoulder, then back to Mallory. "I didn't want to talk out in the hall."

"Well, I don't want to talk now."

"Now or later." His hands lowered, and she didn't miss the way they closed into fists at his side. "It's your choice, but we *will* talk."

At least six feet separated them, but she could swear she could still feel his body against hers. And she felt a heat in her that had little to do with the waning fire in the stove. "There isn't anything to talk about," she said, but her voice held less conviction than she'd wished for.

He came toward her, but stopped within a few feet without touching her again. He ignored her words. "You need to get out of here," he said in a low voice.

She could hear real urgency in his voice, and it shook her to know how passionately he wanted her gone. "Don't start that again. I told you, I don't want your money."

He shook his head. "It's gone past that. You're not safe here any longer."

She swallowed hard. "What are you talking about?"

"When I first saw you at the theater, I knew there'd be problems if Saxon really brought you here. But I never expected how serious the problems would be."

This didn't make sense. "How could you have known who I was when we met at the theater?" *She* hadn't even known abut this job or Saxon Mills then.

"I had a tip that Saxon found a daughter. I got in early from Los Angeles and decided to check it out."

The only people who knew about this charade were Saxon and Henry Welting. Both of them knew this was bogus. "What kind of tip? Who told you about me?"

"That's not important," he said. "What's important is how much trouble you've caused."

"Me?" She pressed one hand to her chest, startled at the rapid thudding of her heart under her palm. "I haven't done anything."

"You've come here. That's enough."

She stood straighter. "Saxon asked me to come here."

"And he didn't give a damn what happened to you once you got here."

She wished she could look him in the eye and tell him he was wrong, but she couldn't. She knew that Saxon probably didn't care what happened to anyone but himself, and he *had* thrown her into the fire, so to speak, without a thought to what it could do to her. "He's a strange man."

"That's an understatement." He frowned. "He's self-centered and egomaniacal. He's brilliant and driven. He uses people and he's dangerous."

She hugged her arms around herself and rubbed her upper arms with the flats of her hands. The chill in the room was growing with each passing moment. "Do you really think he's dangerous?"

"In the sense that he'll get what he wants no matter what it takes." He moved even closer, and Mallory found herself holding her breath. "That means you're expendable."

"I don't understand why you're saying all this. You're in the middle of everything that's going on here. You're angry I'm here, so much so that you offered me a huge amount of money to disappear. Maybe you're like Saxon, using people to get what you want. Seeing them as expendable."

His eyes narrowed, and she knew she'd made a direct hit. Yet it didn't give her any satisfaction, and her first impulse was to take back the words, to make them disappear as if they had never been uttered.

Tony turned from her, but he didn't leave. He went to the stove and held his hands out to what heat radiated from the glowing embers in the grate. "You're probably right. I guess there are some things you just can't walk away from," he said in a low voice.

"Is this what you wanted to talk about?"

He stared at the stove for a long moment, then finally said, "I came here to talk about you, not me."

"If you're going to offer me more money—"

He turned abruptly, the candles in the room playing flickering light over his face and shadowing his lean frame. His slacks were indecently tight, and when he tucked his fingers in the pockets, it only made the material more taut. And it made Mallory's mouth go dry. "I'm not going to offer you any money, but I don't have much time."

Time had no meaning for Mallory since she'd stepped into this house. She'd rushed here to make her appointment, and since then she'd been in a certain limbo, where day and night were interchangeable in shadows and gray light. Unexpectedly, she found herself craving the sun, its heat and its clean light. She looked away from Tony and remembered the wine on the table.

She crossed and poured herself a glass of ruby liquid. The clatter of glass against glass rang on her nerves, but she managed to fill the goblet half-full.

As she put the carafe back on the table, she asked, "Then what is it?"

"I'm really worried."

"I can't help you with business," she said, staring into the wine, at the flicker of candlelight dancing in the liquid.

"It's not that." He hesitated before saying, "I know you won't take money to leave this place."

She closed her eyes and took a drink of the wine. She had fully intended to only sip it, but she found herself drinking half of it before putting the goblet down. She felt its warmth in her middle, then looked at Tony again. "Does it worry you that you won't have the control you want of Saxon's business affairs as long as there's a daughter in the picture?"

He shrugged sharply, but didn't deny it. "That's part of it, but what's got me really worried is Saxon."

"I know, he's egomaniacal, as you said, and—"

"Did you know he thinks Kate's back here with him?"

That stopped her dead. "Kate?"

"Since you've been here, he's been getting confused about what happened years ago, and what's reality now."

"You think he's mentally unstable?"

"Obsessed. Do you know why Kate left him?"

"I know they fought a lot, and they broke up after a big fight."

"I heard that she ran for her life the night she disappeared. He'd flown into one of his rages, and he accused her of flirting with some poor slob she'd never even met before. From what I heard, he tore up the place, she took off, and she never came back."

"And he didn't go looking for her, did he?"

"I think he sent a flunky, maybe even Henry Welting. That man's been around since the Ice Age, but whoever went couldn't find her." He shrugged, testing the material of his shirt. "She was probably too afraid to come back here."

She swallowed the wine as it rose in her throat, then it settled and she was fine. The nausea was gone as quickly as it had come. "You . . . you think he would have hurt her?"

"It sounds as if he tried."

She swallowed again. "Why are you telling me this?"

"If your mother hated Saxon so much that she ran and didn't stop, she must have had a reason. If he accused her of flirting, maybe he wonders about your paternity someway. And if she never tried to get back here, and she didn't even tell him he was a father, maybe she had good reason. She obviously didn't want you to be part of his life."

It was odd that words said about a woman she'd never known brought back a memory she'd all but forgotten about her own mother. *It's just you and me, Mallory, and no one else,* her mother had said deep in the past, her voice touched with bitterness. *We don't need your father. I don't. You don't.*

The impact of the memory was jarring, and the headache from the morning started to nudge at her again. "She said we didn't need him," Mallory breathed, her past mingling unerringly with the fantasy version Saxon Mills had put on her.

"Believe her," he said, coming closer. "You don't need him. And you don't need what he could do to you."

As Tony talked, her stomach began to get queasy. "You make it sound as if he would harm me."

"He's capable of it. God knows he could have hurt Kate." He flicked his gaze over her. "And you look for all the world like your mother's picture. Do you think the past is gone completely, or do you think Saxon could be tangling it up with the present?"

She knew the answer to that, and it chilled her even more. "I know he slips a bit." She tugged at the clip in her hair with an unsteady hand, remembering his reaction to her wearing it up. "He's old. I mean, he's not a young man." She shook her hair out and closed her hand over the clip. "He's bound to fail in some things. But that doesn't mean he really thinks I'm Kate."

"He's already mistaken you for Kate, hasn't he?"

She looked away, gripping the clip, and made a buffer of distance between herself and Tony by going to the windows.

"Did he mistake you for Kate?" he asked.

She shrugged as she used her free hand to tug the heavy curtains back to expose the growing darkness of early evening through windows sheeted with rain. It took her back to see a strange pattern in the glass, the heavy lead distorting the grayness and rain, making odd twinkling patterns that flared into brilliant colors. She blinked quickly, and they vanished as if they had never been.

"Well, did he?" Tony asked from right behind her, jarring her.

The material of the drapes slipped from her hand as she turned. He was so close she could almost feel his body heat through her sweater and jeans. "I'm sorry. What did you say?"

He frowned. "Did Saxon mix you up with Kate?"

In the dimness of the room, Tony seemed to be part of the shadows, except for a strange hazy glow around him when she looked right at him. "Yes, he did."

"What happened?"

She closed her eyes tightly for a moment, then looked back at Tony. No glow, no halo, just his dark intensity right in front of her. "He was angry. He thought I was Kate, and I think he thought I was going to leave him."

"Do it. Leave him and get out of here," Tony said in a low voice.

She knew her part and what she should say, but she had to force out the words as she turned to face him. "But he's my father."

The words hung in the silence between them. Then she saw a flash of pain cross his face. "He could hurt you."

She moved away from Tony toward the bed, and she touched the post, her fingertips feeling the silkiness of the wood and the delicate engravings in it. The carving was beautiful, and she'd never noticed it before. "He...he wouldn't," she said with a degree of distraction.

There was no escape from Tony. He came to her again, and when he touched her shoulder, she almost jumped out of her skin. The clip flew out of her hand, clattering on the floor. Tony stooped and picked it up, then offered it back to her, but this time the matching clip, the one she thought she had lost in the stables, was on his palm, too.

"I found it after you left," he said.

She stared at them, shocked that she couldn't quite make herself take them from him. He must have thought she was ignoring his offer, and he turned, tossing them onto the bedside table. Then he was back in front of her, and he reached out, touching her chin with the tips of his fingers. "Don't treat this lightly. Saxon would hurt you, and I don't want that to happen."

She closed her eyes, the sensations at his touch so overwhelming that she couldn't move. She could feel the tip of each finger on her skin, could almost sense the whorls of his fingerprints. "*You* want me gone."

"I want you safe."

She opened her eyes to meet his dark gaze, her attention riveted on the spot where he touched her. "You want control of the businesses."

"I do, but I'm not like my father that way. I don't want anyone hurt." His fingers traced the line of her jaw. "Especially you."

Her tongue touched her lips, and she felt vaguely dizzy. "You think Saxon would do something?"

"I think anyone in this house is capable of *doing something* to take the threat of your inheritance away."

"Anyone?" She stared at him, unable to stop the remembrance of the moments just past when she thought he was going to harm her. The fear she'd felt was gone, the edges blurred and soft, but the image was still in her mind.

"Anyone," he whispered, and the silence in the room was total.

There were no sounds of rain or wind or lightning, just the low hissing of the dying fire and her own breathing. "Tony, I'm not here to threaten anyone." She had to concentrate on choosing words, her ability to think clearly fading more and more with each passing moment. "I'm really not."

His hand moved to cup her neck, its heat on the nape filling her with a startling degree of comfort. She couldn't remember experiencing that sensation for so long that she wondered if she ever had. She wanted to rest her head against his heart, feel his arms around her and lose herself in it, to rest and not think, to be held and not have to wonder when it would stop or worry about pain that would come sooner or later.

"Then for God's sake, leave," he whispered. His touch on her trembled slightly. "Nothing you can get here is worth what could happen to you."

"You're . . . you're exaggerating," she breathed as his image seemed to float in front of her. He had to be exaggerating.

"I wish I was." His eyes searched her upturned face, then, as if he could look into her soul and see her need, he gently eased her toward him.

In a single heartbeat, all of her needs were answered when his arms circled her and he drew her against him. She lost herself in the heat and strength and the feeling of his heart pounding against her cheek. Closing her eyes, she barely kept tears from falling and wondered when she'd gotten so needy. When had she felt so vulnerable?

Every moment of rightness she'd known fleetingly in her life came back in a rush, mingling and flowing together until it solidified into something so overwhelming that Mallory didn't dare move. She didn't even dare focus on it in case it dissolved and she discovered this was a dream.

The world spun, and she knew if she wished for anything, she'd have it. It was magical, and Tony was her magician. When he eased her back to look at her, she met his gaze, and she could feel the world slowly turning on its ear. When Tony lowered his head and found her lips with his, she knew her wish was coming true.

The kiss in the stables had been like a lightning bolt searing through her, but this caress was like a slow-burning fire. From the moment of contact, it grew and grew until it burned white-hot through her. She moved closer, circling his neck with her arms, straining toward him as the feeling of his body branded her.

She had never felt life so fully, been so aware of everything, down to the texture of his hair under her hands, the way he breathed, his taste, the angles of his body against her. When his hands cupped her bottom, pulling her up against him, she knew a joy that threatened to explode in her. She felt his desire for her, the evidence that he wanted her as much as she wanted him, and she arched toward it, her staggering need for this man a living thing in her.

Somehow he shifted with her, and the next thing she knew, they were on the bed, with Tony over her. His knees were between her legs, and his mouth burned a path along her jaw, to the hollow of her throat. She arched back, exposing her neck to his searching mouth, and sensations exploded within her like skyrockets on the Fourth of July.

When his hand found its way under her top and his fingers splayed on her stomach, she gasped. Breathing became almost impossible as pleasure flowed over her and around her. Her universe became focused on his hand, which played on her stomach, then skimmed higher. The touch on her breast, even through the thin material of her bra, stunned her. The moan she heard was her own, and her body trembled.

"Tony," she whispered, wanting skin against skin. To feel his sleek heat, to know what it felt like to be closer to him than she'd ever been to anyone in her life. She fumbled with her top, tugging at it, and Tony covered her hands with his and eased them back. He shifted to the side, raising himself on one elbow, then, without looking away from Mallory, he slowly began to undo the buttons on the sweater.

Mallory looked up at him, feeling his fingers brushing her skin as he pushed back the wool. She wanted to touch his face, to trace the line of his jaw, to feel the bristling of a new beard beginning, but she couldn't move. Lethargy robbed her of the ability to even touch his lips.

She knew he was gently easing her bra off, then he looked at her, and she heard him whisper, "You're beautiful," but she couldn't speak. It was as if her ability to move had been taken from her.

She felt everything, his touch on her, his fingers teasing her nipples, the swelling of her breasts, the growing tension between her legs. The sensations were clear and bright, almost blinding her. She wanted to tell him to keep touching her, to never stop, to never leave her alone. She wanted to tell him she hated being alone, that she hated the thought that this might all be a dream. She wanted to reach out and pull him over her and feel his weight on her, the strength of him filling her, but she couldn't do anything.

She could see, but not do. She could feel, but not react. When Tony moved over her, his face was so close that she felt the heat of his breath on her skin. "What is it?" he asked, his voice an echo in her mind.

*I want you, I need you,* she thought, but no words would come. *Hold me, love me.* But there was only silence.

Tony moved even closer, his hand at her forehead pressed to her skin, and his face grew dark with a frown. "Mallory?" He said her name less gently. "Mallory?"

She stared at him. Then, without her control, she felt her eyes flutter and close. She was instantly locked in blackness, and the only reality for her was an unnamed terror that sprang from the darkness. A terror she knew would destroy her.

# CHAPTER TEN

Voices.

Floating.

Close.

"Drugs... has to be."

"I should have known. An actress...waitress. Drugs all over..."

"...no doctor...muddy roads..."

"...die? I don't think..."

"...a bad trip...screwed up...what is there...?"

Mallory heard the words coming out of disembodied blackness, mingling with a nightmare of cars rushing at people on rain-soaked streets, the screech of brakes, the smell of burning rubber, Tony standing in front of her in the storm, the tree exploding. The images mixed with the voices, nothing making sense until ever so slowly, she began to understand she was alive.

The voices were still there, coming out of the darkness, pushing back the images until she knew who was talking.

Joyce. "I could have told you about that type."

Lawrence. "You could tell us about a lot of types. Boy, she looks pretty bad."

Myra. "She could have died."

But she wasn't dead. She could feel someone rubbing her hand hard, creating friction.

Saxon. "I owe Tony a lot for finding her in time."

Tony. With her. On the bed. Touching. Kissing. The memory flooded over her, bringing the feeling of finding something, a treasure, something solid in a life that had been bearable at best. Someone to hold to, to anchor her, someone to love.

But Tony wasn't here. She knew, without opening her eyes, that the hand on hers wasn't Tony's. She couldn't sense him. And she knew she was alone... again, the way she'd always been.

As something cold was pressed to her forehead, tears slipped from the corners of her eyes. Alone again.

"Good, good," Saxon murmured. "She's coming around."

Joyce. "God knows what she's been taking."

"Nothing" she wanted to scream, but she couldn't form any words or stop the tears.

Myra. "We will get a doctor as soon as William can get out, but there is no telling how long this storm will last."

"Pitiful," Lawrence muttered. "See what you found, Uncle Saxon? Some druggie who'll cut through your money like a knife through butter."

Drugs? No, never. Then she tasted the bitterness in her mouth and felt the strange fuzziness in her head. What had happened to her? She'd been with Tony. She remembered that. Or did she? Was that a dream? Was the closeness a cruel trick of her mind?

"Lawrence, that's not what's important right now. We need to make sure she's all right, then we can clear this all up."

She tried to open her eyes, to face these people and tell them the truth. But she didn't understand it at all, and the simple effort it would take to open her eyes was too much for her. With a deep sigh, she gave in to the lethargy that tugged at her. And the voices receded into a soft gray.

Myra. "She will sleep for a while."

Lawrence. "Look around and see if we can find what she took."

Joyce. "Her sort probably thinks this is normal."

Saxon. "She'll sleep. Then we'll talk."

And Mallory's last feeling before she fell into a soft, comfortable sleep, was a deep sadness that Tony wasn't there.


Tony stood by the door, silently watching the others. They looked like vultures hovering over Mallory's bed. As soon as he heard Myra say Mallory was falling into a normal sleep, he slipped out of the room and walked away.

With his hands clenched in his pockets, he headed downstairs and into the library. He went directly to the bar, poured himself a shot of whiskey, then tossed it to the back of his throat. The fiery liquid burned down his throat, and he had to stop himself from refilling the glass.

The moment he'd known Mallory had been in real trouble had been terrifying. He'd never expected to feel this way. He'd been so used to doing what had to be done, no matter what the cost, then walking away.

But the moment he'd seen her eyes roll upward and her body look as if it had collapsed, he'd felt something he'd never expected.

He accepted being attracted to her. He accepted the fact that all she had to do was look at him, and he felt a response that was so basic, it was almost beyond his control. He accepted the fact that when he touched her, all bets were off. He didn't accept the fact that in the moment when she'd passed out, he wanted to protect her, to help her . . . to save her.

And when the others had been there, Lawrence being sarcastic, Joyce being judgmental, Saxon being oddly calm, and Myra methodically rubbing Mallory's hand or putting chilled rags on her head, he'd stayed away. He'd watched from the door and waited to make sure she'd be all right, then he'd left.

"Tony?"

He turned and saw Saxon coming into the room. The man looked slightly ashen, and it shocked Tony. Upstairs he'd seemed calm and almost detached, but now he looked bothered and much older. Saxon walked slowly into the room and crossed to a high-backed chair by the curtained windows. As he sank down with a sigh, he looked up at Tony by the bar.

"Pour me a brandy. I'm not going to wait until after dinner."

Tony splashed a healthy portion of brandy in a snifter, then handed it to Saxon. As the elderly man took it, Tony asked, "How is she?"

Saxon was silent until he took a sip of the amber liquid, then he sat back in the chair. "It looks as if she'll be fine. I wish there was a doctor who could get here, but until one can, I think she'll be all right."

Tony exhaled, regretting not pouring himself another drink. "I thought she might not make it."

Saxon rested his snifter on the arm of his chair and closed his eyes. "I know. It scared the hell out of me."

He could almost believe that the old man had been really worried, but that had never been Saxon's style. "It scared the hell out of everyone."

The man shifted and looked back at Tony. "What do you think happened?"

"I don't know. I was going past and—"

Saxon swore, and the brandy sloshed in his snifter. "Stop it. I know you were in the room with her. Now you tell me what happened."

Tony shrugged. The old man knew everything. "We were talking." He ignored Saxon's growing frown. "She got dizzy and then blacked out."

"Did you see her take anything?"

"No, nothing."

Saxon closed his eyes and pinched the bridge of his nose between his thumb and forefinger. "They're saying it's drugs."

Turning to cross to the bar, Tony tossed over his shoulder, "What do you know about her life before you found her?"

"She lived alone. She worked hard. She had nothing. But she wasn't in the gutter, and there was nothing in Henry's files that even hinted that she had a substance-abuse problem."

"Does she have any medical problems?" he asked as he splashed some whiskey in his glass.

"None that Henry found out about."

"Would it make any difference if she did have a drug problem, or some ongoing health problem?" he asked, staring into his glass.

Saxon was silent for so long, Tony finally turned with his drink in his hand. The old man was staring blankly at the shelves opposite his chair while his fingers worried the stem of the brandy snifter.

"Well, would it?" Tony said, trying to prod an answer out of him.

"I'm her father. It shouldn't make a difference, should it?"

"But does it? Is Mallory expendable to you, Saxon?"

The man took a sip of his brandy, then exhaled. "Of course not." He cast Tony a slanted glance. "I'm not your father, Tony. I don't destroy people because of imperfections. And I'm not like you. I don't turn my back on family." He actually chuckled, a rough, rusty sound. "Living proof is me having my so-called family here over the holidays. They're all I've got, Tony, my own small part of immortality."

Tony refused to think that the old man had a heart. That would complicate everything. "Then you're in trouble," he muttered, and downed his drink.

"How about you?"

He looked at Saxon. "You've pretty much summed it up. I turned my back on any family I might have had."

"I meant about you and Mallory."

Tony's hand tightened on his empty glass. "What are you talking about?"

"The stables. Her room. You tell me."

"We've been talking," he said with a shrug.

"Is that all you've been doing?"

He glared at Saxon, hating the old man for cutting to the quick with such ease. "I've been getting to know your daughter, Saxon."

"If you think working on her is going to make me deal differently with you, you're dead wrong. Our business is between the two of us. Mallory has nothing to do with it."

He met the old man's blue gaze, not flinching and not turning away. "She's got everything to do with it. You've seen to that."

"That's my business."

"Damn straight, it is, and you're dangling it in front of the bunch of us like strawberries in front of a donkey."

"And you're running with the rest of them to get it, aren't you?" he asked. "The question is, how far are you willing to go for what you want? And how expendable is Mallory to *you?*"

Tony had never hated anyone like he hated the old man in the chair at that moment. "I'm not you, Saxon."

"No, but you're a Danforth," the man said, hitting the mark.

"Damn you," Tony muttered.

"You're not the first one who damned me."

"And I won't be the last."

The old man lifted his snifter in a mock salute. "Amen to that."

"Saxon, let her go."

He slowly lowered his glass. "Why would I?"

"Maybe because it could be the first decent thing you've done in your life."

Saxon stared down into the snifter. "Don't hold your breath for that to happen."

Tony stared down at the man. "Do it for her."

"I let Kate go," he said softly, moving the snifter to swirl the liquid around and around. "I let her go, and she never came back. She took everything and dropped right off the face of the earth. I'm not going to let that happen again."

"Mallory isn't Kate."

The glass stilled, and the old man's hand tightened on the crystal until his knuckles were bloodless. Then Saxon sat forward and put the glass on the table. "I need to get ready for dinner." He stood without looking at Tony before he started for the door. "Since this emergency threw the schedule off, we're dining at eight."

"Saxon?"

The old man stopped, but didn't turn. "What?"

"She *isn't* Kate."

Saxon cast him a look over his shoulder. "Leave her alone, Tony," he said, then walked out.

Tony watched him go and had to kill the urge to grab something—anything—and throw it after him.

## *December 24*

Mallory woke slowly, coming to consciousness gradually, fumbling with a memory of what happened before she slept.

Tony. He'd been here, in bed with her, kissing, touching. But after that there was no memory. Surely she would have remembered every moment if they'd made love. Surely it would have branded her soul.

She was in bed, but even that didn't make sense. She was filled with a heavy lethargy that made even thinking of opening her eyes an effort. Her hands and feet were tingling, and even without moving, she knew she was very much alone.

Scattered images flew at her, and truth and dreams were all tangled up. Tony, touching, holding, kissing, giving her a pleasure that knew no bounds.... But quickly those images were replaced by frightening memories. Voices that had no faces. Talk of death and drugs.

Everything was so confusing. She didn't know where reality ended and hallucinations began. She didn't know if she'd been in her bed all the time, or if Tony had been here. She didn't know if Saxon had been standing over her talking, Myra putting something cold on her head. Someone rubbing her hands.

Maybe she never woke from the first nightmare, and everything else had been part of that. Was she still in San Francisco, and Saxon Mills was a figment of her imagination? Maybe Tony was part of the fantasy, the desire in her to find someone, to have a closeness she had never known before.

Maybe it was all her imagination. And the thought that none of it had been real brought a pain that was startling. When she heard a soft whimpering sound, it took her a moment to realize she was making it. The next instant she heard a shuffling noise, and she knew she wasn't alone. Even without opening her eyes, she knew someone was there, watching, waiting.

"Mallory?"

Tony. She managed to open her eyes to a room that was dark except for the glow from candles near the bed. Tony was over her, dark and large, with shadows as his mantle.

"That's it. Open your eyes."

"What...wh...?" Her mouth was so dry she could barely form words.

"Shh," he whispered, and his touch on her head startled her, a soft stroke at her temple. "You're going to be all right. You've just been sleeping for a long time."

She looked up at him, her desire to love this man overlapping with a fear she had no name for. "I...I..." She coughed softly. "I don't understand."

Tony tugged the comforter higher on her, as if she were a little child he was tucking into bed. "No one does."

As he sank down by her on the side of the bed, she asked, "What happened?"

"You tell me."

She felt ridiculously weak, and tears were far too close to the surface, fed by frustration and anxiety. "Tony, don't. I can't." She fought the burning tears, but she couldn't stop them from sliding down her cheeks. "Please, tell me."

With shattering gentleness, Tony touched her cheek, smoothing the tear with the tip of his finger. "Do you do drugs?"

So she *had* heard that. "No. I... Once I tried, but they made me feel terrible. I never did it again."

"Do you have some ongoing illness that you take medication for?"

"No."

"Well, something made you pretty sick."

She clenched her hands on the comforter, crushing the fine fabric. "Tell me."

"We were here, together, and the next thing I knew, you were unconscious. When I couldn't wake you, I went to get help. The storm's washed out the roads, so no doctor could get through, but Myra has some background in nursing. She knew what to do, and you finally fell into a natural sleep. You've been asleep for almost sixteen hours."

"What?"

"You needed it."

"I thought I was dreaming."

His fingers stilled on her cheek. "It wasn't a dream. It was a nightmare."

The perfect word. "I know. I just don't know why I got sick."

"Maybe you aren't sick. Maybe someone was trying to make it look as if you were using drugs."

She cringed at that thought. "Why would they do that?"

"Saxon hates imperfection. He hates weakness. You figure it out."

"That's . . . that's paranoid."

"Maybe. Maybe not. What's that old saying? Just because you're paranoid, it doesn't mean everyone isn't out to get you."

She would have laughed at that if she hadn't felt so unsteady or if the fear she'd felt since walking into this house hadn't been growing. "I didn't take anything."

"You ate and drank with Saxon."

"That was at lunch."

"It's the last thing you ate or drank. Two and two makes four, if you add it up right."

She shifted, easing herself up onto one elbow, and she brushed her hair back from her face. She felt an unsettling clamminess on her skin. "That's crazy. Why would Saxon do anything like that to me?"

"I don't know. Forget I said it." He stood. "If a person's around this family long enough, they tend to get a bit unbalanced. I'll check in on you later."

"You don't have to. I'll be fine."

"I'll check," he said.

With an intimacy that should only have come after years of closeness, he bent over her and eased her back into the pillows, then carefully tugged the comforter over her.

She looked up at him and asked a question that had been teasing the edges of her mind since she'd woken to find him here with her. "Tony?"

"What?" he asked, straightening up.

"Earlier, you and me... I mean, before this all happened, we were together and we..." She touched her tongue to lips that were cold now. "Did we... I mean, I don't remember, and I..."

He bent over her again, coming so close that she felt as if he filled up her world. "No, we didn't. If we had, I assure you, you wouldn't have to ask." He smiled, the expression akin to the sun cutting through the gray dullness that shrouded this house. Then he touched his lips to her forehead in a chaste caress, yet one that seemed to touch her soul. As he drew back, he whispered, "Sleep. I'll come back up after lunch."

"Why are you here now?"

"I wanted to make sure you were all right."

That didn't answer her question, but she left it at that as he turned and started for the door. She bit her lip to keep from asking him to stay, to not leave her alone.

When he got to the door, he turned and looked at her through the shadows. "Don't trust anyone in this house, Mallory."

"What about you?"

"Trust yourself." Then he was gone, the door closing softly behind him.

Mallory sank back in the bed, then rolled onto her side and pulled her knees to her stomach. She stared at the fire through the grate in the stove, but the heat couldn't touch the core of coldness deep inside her. She hadn't taken anything. And now that her mind was clearing, she knew something else had happened. She closed her eyes. Saxon. Why would he harm her? The answer was there as quickly as the question formed.

He hated Kate. She looked like Kate. She snuggled deeper in the bed, tired and lethargic, but strangely not able to sleep. Closing her eyes, she tried to make herself relax, to drift into that world halfway between waking and sleeping.

Just as she felt herself letting go, she sensed someone behind her. She hadn't heard anyone come in. Maybe she had drifted off for a moment. Shifting, she turned, but as she looked behind her, the room was empty. She pushed herself up, looked around and knew she wasn't alone.

As she eased back in the bed, she stared into the shadows. "Tony?" she whispered.

But the only answer was the whisper of rain against the windows and the hissing of the fire. Then she tentatively said, "Kate?" Maybe the others had been right—Kate haunted this house. A house she ran from in life, she lingered in, in death.

Mallory pushed those thoughts away, the very idea of death making her shiver. And she wasn't sleepy. Whatever had happened left her tired, but sixteen hours of sleep seemed to have been enough. She shifted and felt her clothes catch on the bedding.

She needed to change, to get out of the clothes she'd worn for over a day. Slowly, she eased herself up, then put her legs over the side of the bed. She sat there for a long time watching the fire in the stove and testing her body. Her head was clearer, the thought process more distinct, and the strange mixture of dreams and facts was beginning to sort itself out.

She stood with the help of one hand pressed flat on the bed. Her legs were vaguely unsteady, but when she let go of her hold on the bed, she was fine. She headed for the bathroom, picking up her robe on the way, then started a bath.

In ten minutes, she felt almost normal. If she tried she could block out Tony's words, and she could focus on this whole thing being a job. When she went back into the bedroom, wearing her robe, she sank down on the side of the bed. Swallowing, she felt a tightness in her throat, but that was it.

She spotted wine on the table, white wine this time, and she got up to pour herself a glass. She took a sip to ease the dryness in her mouth, and as she put the goblet back on the side table, she remembered Tony had said he was going down to dinner. The house would be empty with everyone in the dining hall or the kitchen.

And she wanted to move around a bit. She dressed quickly in jeans and a sweatshirt, then pushed her feet into running shoes and left the room. The hallway was deserted, and she couldn't hear anything at all as she walked toward the stairs. She started down, running her hand along the banister as she descended. When she was halfway down, she heard voices and stopped.

"I'm telling you, she's on drugs," Joyce was saying somewhere below, her voice raised.

Mallory looked down and realized the door was open on the far side of the hallway. The doors had never been open before, but now she could see thick red carpeting and overstuffed furniture in a deep hunter green. She eased down a few more steps and listened.

"The thing is, what should you do, Uncle Saxon?"

"Whatever I decide to do," Saxon said, "I'll do."

"She might be your daughter, but God knows how she's lived in the city. You could have brought a psychopath into this family."

Mallory waited for the laughter, the recognition of the absurdity of the statement, but she didn't expect Tony to say, "You said that Henry had her checked out pretty thoroughly, didn't you?"

"Of course he did—as much as he could."

"Maybe he needs to dig a bit deeper," Tony said.

Mallory felt a sickness in her middle as she listened. Tony had been the one to be there when she woke up—he'd listened, and he'd seemed to care. But he was just like the others, looking for her Achilles' heel. Then he'd strike.

She pressed a hand to her middle and a sharp metallic taste rose in her throat. Gripping the railing, she took a deep breath, but instead of making things better, it only made her head feel light, as the voices again become audible.

"She didn't faint. She was out of it. Next thing you know, she'll O.D. on the stuff. How's that going to look?"

"Leave it to you, Joyce, to worry about appearances. What about if she doesn't O.D., and she gets control of this family's assets?" Lawrence's voice was becoming strident. "She could take everything and leave a pile of ashes."

The sickness rose in Mallory in waves, and she swallowed over and over again. She had to get back to her room, away from this before anyone saw her. But when she tried to turn, the world began to slip away.

"Don't borrow trouble," Saxon said, his voice louder now.

"No, he's right, Saxon," Tony said, and Mallory could have sworn he was coming closer. "She's an unknown, someone you don't even know if you can trust."

But she couldn't focus. The images in front of her were doubled, then blurred. She twisted to regrip the railing and pull herself back up to the top, and she knew it was happening again. But this time Tony wasn't lying with her in bed.

"Mallory?"

As if she had conjured him up, she heard Tony say her name from below. But when she turned, her feet slipped on the step. She grabbed for the smooth wood of the banister, but before she could grip it, she was tumbling downward. Her hands closed on air, and her right foot struck something hard. The world blurred and spun, and screams that rang in her ears, echoed with her own.

# CHAPTER ELEVEN

In a world gone mad, time slowed to freeze-frames. Mallory saw the carpet-covered steps coming for her head, the marble of the foyer right below her. But when she stretched out her hands to break her fall, she hit something soft and yielding. There was no jarring impact with cold tiles, and no searing pain.

For what could have been a second or an eternity, she was caught and held. Strong hands stilled her plunge inches from impact with the marble, easing her down the rest of the way until she was safely on the bottom step. She sat awkwardly, someone supporting her by the shoulders.

When she looked up, she saw Tony, a blurred, distorted figure, his dark eyes overly huge in his face, his jaw long and heavy. When he spoke, his voice sounded as if someone had put him on slow speed, a deep echo that rang in her mind.

"Steady, steady," he said.

"Steady," she echoed, her voice slurred, and she had the silly idea he was talking to a high-strung horse.

With her hands lying limply in her lap, she heard herself giggling. A horse. Just like a horse. Tony shook her, but it didn't stop the hysterical laughter or the way the world was making monsters out of normal people.

Joyce was over Tony's shoulder, a blob of green, sort of like a Christmas tree with a gargoyle head. The giggling only increased. And Lawrence, a weasel with a sharp face and long nose. Saxon, tall and haggard, with a shock of white hair above a face with eyes that seemed to glow red.

The laughter died and fear rose in Mallory. Prey. That's what she was. Prey for these monsters. Then she looked at Tony and wished he didn't look so grim. If only he'd smile again. Just once. That's all she needed. A smile from him.

But what she got was a low oath and a, "Damn it, what did you take?"

"Take?" she repeated in a high, silly voice. "Take?"

"I told you to check out her room," Lawrence the weasel said, his voice sounding as if he were lost in a long tunnel of fog.

"Why didn't you?" Joyce the Christmas tree asked sharply.

Mallory held up a hand, not caring that it was shaking. "I never took anything," she whispered. And as her hand fell limply, she looked at Tony and collapsed into his arms.

When Mallory woke the next time, she was alone. The fire in the stove was out, candlelight danced on the walls and ceiling, and the blankets had been pulled up to her chin. Unlike the first time, she woke with a start and was instantly aware of what was going on. She remembered the stairs, the dizziness, and Tony catching her before she hit the marble floor.

It had happened again. She tugged her hand free of the blankets and pressed it to her forehead, her skin clammy again. And this time she hadn't eaten or drunk anything. She'd been in this room. She'd been alone after Tony left. She'd bathed and changed and ...

She raised herself on one elbow and looked at the table. She'd taken a drink of wine. But the carafe and goblets were gone, replaced by a jug of water and short, fat glasses. She remembered drinking a half glass the first time, and this time just a sip or two for her dry mouth.

She sank back in the bed. There had to have been something in the wine. There was no other explanation for what happened to her. But what had it been doctored with? And who had done it? Anyone could have brought it in the first time when she'd been with Saxon. The second time she'd been asleep.

It could have been Joyce, anxious to have something to hold over her. Or Lawrence—anything to make Mallory look worse in Saxon's eyes than he did.

She swallowed hard, the now-familiar metallic taste on her tongue. Slowly, she eased herself up until she was sitting in the middle of the bed. Chilly air ran over her bare arms, and as the blankets slipped down, she realized someone had dressed her in the long, white T-shirt.

A soft shuffling sound came from outside the door, and Mallory braced herself for someone coming into the room. But nothing happened. She leaned forward and looked at the door. "Hello?" she called out, halfway wishing it would be Tony, halfway wishing nothing more than to be left alone to make sense out of everything.

She was about to sit back in the bed, when the candle flickered as if caught in an errant draft of air. Then she saw a flashing movement at the base of the door. She leaned farther forward, bracing herself with her hands pressed flat on the bedding. She could almost make out something on the floor, something light and small.

She pushed back the covers, then eased out of bed, using the post to steady herself before she crossed the room barefoot. She dropped to her haunches by the door and saw a folded piece of paper on the floor. Picking it up, she went back to the bed, near the candlelight, and opened it. The paper was fine, like parchment, and its ocher color made the block letters scratched in runny blue ink stand out even more than they would have normally.

*"KATE DIED AND SO WILL YOU."*

She stared at the paper, assimilating the fact that everything she'd suspected before was true. It wasn't a product of her paranoia or her imagination. Someone was trying to get her out of the way, no matter what it took—even threatening her life.

She slowly folded the expensive paper with shaking hands, almost as unsettled by her impulse to go to Tony and get him to help her, as by the threat. She knew she couldn't go to him. There wasn't anyone she could go to except Saxon. That knowledge only underscored the fact she had no business being here, and a sense of isolation flooded over her, leaving her cold and shaky.

She tossed the note onto the bed, hating even the feel of it in her hands, then dressed quickly in jeans, a heavy sweater and her old running shoes. Leaving her hair loose, she crossed and eased back her door. Once she made sure the hallway was empty, she silently slipped out and headed for Saxon's suite. When there was no answer, she tested the latch, felt it click, and the door swung quietly back.

Heat from a blazing fire in the hearth touched her chilled skin, making her shiver as she looked into the room. The shadows were partially dispelled by a half-dozen candles set on the dresser, both nightstands and the desk.

"Saxon?" she called softly. "Saxon?"

No answer. She stepped inside, quietly shut the door, then turned to look around. The sudden chime of a wall clock by the door startled her, and she turned. It was eleven o'clock. As the last chime died out, she called, "Saxon?"

A door beyond the desk was open, and flickering light showed through it. She crossed and looked into a huge bathroom almost the size of the bedroom. The light of several candles glinted off the marble and porcelain, as well as the gold fixtures. But this room was as empty as the other had been.

She turned, trying to think of what to do, and when she saw the fire, she knew she wasn't going anywhere. She was safe and warm here. She would wait for Saxon to come up for bed, then decide what to do. But as she started for the chairs by the hearth, she passed the desk, stopping when she saw the framed picture again, sitting on the polished surface.

She reached down and touched the cool glass that protected it. Kate. The start of all of this. She was truly beautiful, the way Mallory thought her mother might have been if she hadn't been so tired and worn-out from life. She squinted at the picture, startled that if she narrowed her eyes just so, Kate resembled her mother, just happier and younger than the fuzzy memories Mallory still had.

She shook her head, knowing she was going off the deep end, but it suddenly hit her that except for a quirk of fate, this could be her reality. It could be true that Saxon was her father, that these people hated her for what she could do to them, that they wanted her dead.

As she jerked her hand back, she accidentally knocked the dish the candle sat on, and the candle teetered, then settled upright. But hot wax drops had scattered on the desk's polished surface.

"Damn," she muttered, quickly opening the top drawer of the desk to find something to blot up the wax before it marred the finish. But when she looked in the drawer, she forgot all about the wax. Stationery and envelopes were neatly arranged in the shallow drawer, and as Mallory lifted the top sheet of the parchment paper, she knew it was the same paper the threatening note had been written on.

Lying beside the stationery was an old-fashioned fountain pen. Blue ink darkened the tip and a drop had stained the bottom of the drawer.

The paper fell from Mallory's hand. Saxon was crazy. He hadn't brought her here to bait his family and Tony. He'd brought her here to replace Kate and to take out his revenge for what Kate had done to him years ago. Mallory slid the drawer shut and, ignoring the hardening wax on the desk top, she headed for the door.

She had to get out of here so she could think. With her heart hammering, she opened the door, looked into the hall, then cautiously stepped out. When she didn't see anyone, she headed for the stairs. As she gripped the rail, she heard muted Christmas music, as if coming from behind closed doors. Holiday cheer seemed doubly galling to her right now.

She started down the stairs, and when she quietly stepped onto the marble floor of the foyer, which was lit by candles, she headed to the front door. As she touched the cold latch, she heard voices raised over the music, but she couldn't understand what they were saying. The others must be having their Christmas Eve celebration.

Glancing back over her shoulder, she couldn't see anything. Quickly, she eased open the front door and stepped out into a misty, cold night. The chill cut through her clothes, but the air was fresh and clean, and behind rolling clouds in the sky, there was a suggestion of moonlight. It gave enough illumination for her to see where she was going.

She hurried down the stairs, out from under the portico and off to the left. She needed to think, to sort through everything and decide what she was going to do. She pushed her hands in the pockets of her jeans, wishing she'd thought to grab a jacket before leaving, but she wasn't about to go back inside for one. As she looked up at the clouded heavens, she felt the cool mist brush her face.

She knew where she was going—the one place on this property that she felt as if she could be alone, where no one would be watching her. She followed a stone pathway around the perimeter of the house, passing the lower windows lit by flickering candles. Then she stepped out onto the drive that lead to the stables.

She was startled by the sound of a door opening close by and the ringing of feet hitting solid ground. She took off at a jog toward the stables through the misty night. With each step she took, she knew that she wasn't going to stay here any longer. Now that the rain had eased off, she could leave. She would manage without the money if Saxon refused to pay her. One way or another she would get her car out of the ditch.

Yet as she made a decision that should have been liberating, that should have given her immense relief, all she could really think about was Tony and never seeing him again. Her world certainly wouldn't intersect with his on any level. And once he knew she wasn't Saxon's heir, he wouldn't have a reason to seek her out.

That thought made her sad. Maybe she'd been kidding herself, letting her imagination run wild, but for a while, for a brief glitch in time, she'd let herself think that maybe she'd finally found an anchor. But it was all built on lies and deceptions.

She stopped running and settled into a quick walk. Then she heard the sound of a horse whinnying in the stables ahead. What little light there was from the clouded sky showed the slickness of the slate roof and the deep arch of the central breezeway.

As she neared the top of the circle, she heard someone walking behind her, and that only drove her to the safety of the stables more quickly. She approached the big double doors, grabbed the latch and tugged. The huge door eased back enough for her to slip inside and out of the chilly breeze. She passed the stalls with the horses and went down to the end of the aisle, where she opened another door and looked inside. She'd found a tack room with tiny windows set high in stone walls.

As her eyes adjusted to the deep shadows, she could see piles of loose hay, shelves and racks that held all sorts of grooming tools, saddles, blankets and other tack, and clothes that had been tossed in a pile near the door. The scent of leather, hay and horses mingled pleasantly in the damp air.

She stepped inside and picked up a couple of saddle blankets, then spread them on the loose hay under the windows and dropped down on the makeshift seat. She took several calming breaths and relished the sense of being alone. There was no feeling of being watched in here at all.

When she heard the scuffing of feet in the hay-littered aisle outside the room, she readied herself to run if she had to. But as she saw a silhouette appear in the doorway, she didn't need a light to know it was Tony.

Relief mingled with a real pleasure that he was here, until she realized that there was nothing he could do.

"I thought I'd find you down here," he said, his voice soft in the shadows.

Her heart lurched. "Were you looking for me?"

"I went to check and see how you were, and you were gone."

"I just wanted to be alone."

"That's why I came down here."

As her eyes adjusted more, she could see he was dressed in dark clothes, from a high-necked shirt to tight pants and a Windbreaker. A man of darkness, but a man who could bring light into her world with a simple touch. Or just by being here.

"I had to think about things."

"What things?"

She wished she could just tell him everything, but she couldn't. Not yet. "About Saxon." That was true enough.

He never moved from the door. "What about him?"

"I don't think he's balanced."

"Mentally balanced?"

"Yes."

"And if he's not?"

She heard the horses stirring in the far stalls and realized that rain was tapping on the roof. "I . . . I don't know."

"Will you leave?"

She pulled her knees to her chest and wrapped her arms around her legs. "I might have to. But one way or another I'll survive."

"I had my doubts when I saw you falling down those stairs."

She shivered and hugged her legs more tightly. "I thought I heard your voice, but everything was so distorted."

"You were about ten stairs from the bottom, and when I looked up and saw you, you just tumbled forward. You fell right into my arms and started to laugh." She could see the sharp movement of a shrug. "Not that I don't like women falling at my feet, but you scared the hell out of me."

"It scared the hell out of me, too," she whispered.

"Saxon tore apart your room looking for drugs while you were passed out."

She closed her eyes for a long moment before looking back at Tony. "There aren't any drugs. At least, not that I took knowingly."

"What does that mean?"

"Someone's really trying to get rid of me, to get me out of the house and out of Saxon's life."

Tony moved toward her and dropped to his haunches in front of her. "What?"

"It's all so crazy, but I know someone had to put something in the wine in my room. I drank it before the first episode."

"You did."

"The second time, I just took a bit, not as much, and it wasn't as bad. I don't know. But I do know that I didn't take any drugs."

"You could get the wine tested, I suppose."

"It's gone. There's water there now."

He exhaled. "Is that why you're out here hiding?"

She looked at him, killing the urge to reach out and hold on to him for dear life. "No. I got a note in my room. It said that Kate died and so would I."

"Where is it?"

"It's in my room. I left it on the bed."

He touched her arm. "It's time for you to leave, no matter how bad the roads are."

The chill in the stable was growing as quickly as the sound of rain outside was. "I know. I'll go as soon as it's light." She shivered. "I can walk out, if I have to."

"I'll go back to the house with you, and you can lock yourself in your room until morning."

"No. I'm not going back to the house...not yet. I never feel as if I'm alone there. Have you felt that, as if you're being watched all the time?"

"You probably are. I'm sure everyone's waiting for you to trip up."

"No, I mean when you're totally alone and you can feel eyes on the back of your neck." She covered his hand with hers, relishing the heat in the touch. "I know that sounds weird, but I mean it."

"It's in your blood to be weird, but that doesn't mean it's not true."

She closed her eyes. "It's nothing to do with my blood." She bit her lip, then opened her eyes to look right at Tony. "I just wish I'd never come here."

He watched her closely. "Then why did you come?"

She shrugged, the lies harder and harder to form around this man. "I had to see Saxon." That was the truth. "I couldn't pass that up."

"I understand. With Saxon, you thought you could have everything you never had."

"It's not that." She trembled when a cold draft invaded the tack room. "It's freezing. It never got this cold in the city."

He let go of her, breaking a contact that she realized she needed desperately right now. But he didn't leave her. She could make out his shadowy form moving around the room. Then she heard the hissing of a match being struck and saw Tony's face exposed by the flare of the flame. Dark eyes, deep shadows at his jaw and throat, and something so endearing to her that it took away her ability to breathe for a moment.

She watched him carefully light a kerosene lantern that hung beside an electrical outlet in the ceiling. Then he shook out the match, and the glow from the lamp pushed back the shadows. Tony crossed and closed the door to the room, threw a bolt, then came back to Mallory. He crouched in front of her.

"You can stay here. There's a heavy bolt on the door on the inside. I'll go back and lock your room so no one will know you're not there. That way you'll be safe here until morning. Then we'll get you out of here, safe and sound."

She could hear the wind buffeting against the stone walls. *Safe.* She wouldn't be if he left her. She knew that as surely as she knew she didn't want to be alone tonight. "They can get into my room," she said as she shivered.

Tony moved to sit by her on the blankets over the hay. When he slipped his arm around her shoulders and pulled her to his side, it seemed so right. She closed her eyes and rested her head in the hollow of his shoulder, relishing his closeness and wishing it would never end. "Maybe, but if it's quiet in there, they won't have a need to," he murmured, his voice rumbling pleasantly against her cheek. "Saxon won't bother, and as long as the others don't think you're wandering around in a drugged daze, they won't bother, either. Besides, your family's probably all in bed by now."

"Saxon isn't."

"That man wanders around at night. He always has. But he mostly goes through the new construction, probably trying to figure out what to build next."

"He really is strange."

"I won't argue with that, even though he's family to you."

"So much for a loving family," she breathed.

"Mallory, a family isn't always loving. That's not in the rules. Otherwise, there wouldn't be any need for wills and gatherings like this one."

"Your family wasn't very loving, was it?"

"My mother tried." His hold on her tightened. "But she wasn't any match for my father. I think she died from a broken heart. My father was self-centered and autocratic to the extreme."

"So you just turned your back on him?"

"That isn't exactly the way it was. I had a choice after my mother died—to do what my father wanted or get out. So I chose to walk. When my father died in prison, I grieved—not for the man he was, but for the man I wished he'd been."

She felt her heart ache for Tony. While she'd been daydreaming about a make-believe father who would rush to find her and claim her for his own, he'd been living the reality of a father who couldn't be a father. "What a horrible choice to have to make."

"It was rough. I know it's going to be hard for you to find out where you can be in Saxon's life."

She closed her eyes as his fingers began to massage her shoulder and arm. "I don't know if I could ever turn away from my family." She almost said, *If I had one,* but bit her lip to stop it.

If Tony was her family, she would never be able to turn her back on him. That thought struck her with staggering power, but it didn't stop there. As his fingers moved on her, kneading at her tight muscles, she knew that if she loved him it would be impossible for her to ever walk away from him.

*Love?* The word had had little meaning for her for most of her life. But now it was a word that held magic and fear, a sensuous mixture that brought into play emotions she had never explored before. She closed her eyes. She knew that if she let herself, she could love this man completely and forever. If she just let go.

She must have tensed, because Tony whispered, "It's all right. You don't have to do anything until the morning."

This was crazy. He didn't even know who she was. And he'd done nothing but try to get her out of here. He'd used everything from anger, to money, to touching her soul. She bit her lip hard. He'd touched her soul. "Yes, until the morning," she echoed.

"Until then, you just have to stay warm and stay here."

Warm? She felt as if she were next to a blazing fire, a fire that could consume her if she let herself touch it. And she was quickly losing her ability to move away from it. She sat very still, but when she felt Tony shift and rest his cheek on her bent head, she knew there was no turning back where this man was concerned.

She pulled away enough to look up at him, and words that she didn't even know were forming came out before she could stop them. "Stay here with me?"

He looked down at her, and his hand touched her cheek tentatively. "I need to get back so they won't come looking for both of us."

"They won't go anywhere until the storm lets up." She was very still. "Stay here, please."

He laughed, a rough unsteady sound. "That's a tempting invitation. I'd hate to turn it down."

His voice faltered as she moved closer, and she knew there'd be more to deal with in the morning than just leaving this place. But right now, morning seemed an eternity away. "Then don't."

With a low moan, he lowered his head, and his lips claimed hers. Mallory expected pleasure from the touch, the memory of the last kiss clear and fresh, despite what had happened later. But she wasn't prepared to feel every atom of her body respond, every particle of her being become so attuned to the man that it was as if she breathed with him, and her heart beat with his.

She arched toward him, circling his neck with her arms, holding him tightly as his mouth plundered hers. His invasion was hot and deep, and she welcomed it with a frenzy that was terrifying. Yet it felt so right, as if she had been created just for this moment in time with this man.

And as his hands explored her, tugging and pushing at the heavy wool and the denim, she knew that she loved Tony. It was that simple and that complicated. It was a love that defied any explanation, any logic. She loved him, and as the truth of that thought sank into her soul, she gloried in it.

# CHAPTER TWELVE

When Tony sat back from Mallory, the loss of contact was wrenching, until she saw him stand and strip off his clothes. In the soft glow of the lantern overhead, she saw Tony before her, his sleek body exciting and stunning. Then he was back with her, his body heat burning through her clothes. Frantically, she tugged at her sweater, trying to free herself from the last barrier that kept them apart.

Tony covered her hands, gently taking over, slipping her sweater over her head and tossing it back with his clothes. Then his fingers were at the waist of her jeans, sliding down the zipper, and he eased the denim off her hips, then freed it from her legs.

Mallory was vaguely aware of the storm's fury building again. She was focused on her own frenzied need for this man, to feel him touch her and know her, and to have him become one with her.

She tugged at her bra, loosening the clasp, then it was gone, and the cold air in the room barely touched her nakedness before Tony was over her and around her. His body heat filtered into her, and the world consisted of only the two of them and this moment, this beat of her heart, and the knowledge that she had never loved a man the way she loved Tony.

His touch skimmed over her, tracing a pattern on her back, then going lower to cup her hip and pull her onto her side to face him. She wrapped her leg over his thigh and pressed a palm to his bare chest, loving the feeling of his rapid, strong heartbeat. His hand traced the sweep of her waist, then trailed up her side, curving slowly around to her front.

She stopped breathing and concentrated on his touch. Then, when she thought she would cry out, his hand cupped her breast. She swelled in his caress, her nipple hardening instantly, and exquisite pleasure coursed through her. Arching her head, she offered herself to him, and the next instant his hand was replaced by his lips. His tongue teased her nipples, first one, then the other, tightening them to an unbearable level of ecstasy, and fire shot through her, centering in her belly.

When his lips left her breast, she cried out, then sucked in a startled breath when she felt him tasting her stomach and trailing his tongue down her abdomen to the flimsy silk of her bikini panties. Tony shifted. He raised his head as one hand touched her swollen breast and the other gently worked its way under the elastic of her panties.

She opened her eyes and gazed down at Tony, their eyes meeting as he slid her panties down off her hips. He whispered, "You're beautiful," as his hand moved to her core. For a long moment, he simply rested his hand against her. "I need you," he said in a low, rough voice.

She reached out and touched his cheek with the tips of her fingers. "Please, love me," she breathed.

As if her words were magic, Tony started moving his hand on her, making circles with his palm. Instantly, she felt sensations that threatened to explode in her. She gasped, arching back, closing her eyes, trying to absorb the exquisite torture of his touch. Instinctively, she began to move with him, circles on circles, building a glory in her that was so unique it almost brought tears to her eyes.

When Tony tested her with one finger, then two, she cried out again, the world swelling into sensations and pleasures that were almost painful.

"No," she gasped. "No." And Tony stopped, the cessation of movement agony for her.

She looked down at him, his face sheened with dampness, his eyes filled with a fire that was a mirror image of her own. Then she reached out for him with trembling hands, needing to hold on to him before she let herself go. "Please," she sobbed, tears finally touching her cheeks.

Tony came to her, shifting over her, bracing himself with one hand and wiping at her tears with the other. "Mallory, you don't have—"

She couldn't speak past the tightness in her throat, so she simply framed his face with both of her hands and lifted her hips to him in invitation. Without another word, Tony was there, his legs between hers, his strength pressed against her. With a low moan, he touched her with silk and heat and entered her.

As he filled her, she wrapped her legs around his hips, and with his first thrust, she found herself moving under him, arching higher and higher. Her hips met his, and she heard herself begging for him to go deeper and deeper. With each stroke, she knew she was coming closer to a point where she'd surely cease to exist and she'd become one with him.

Her body began to shake, and she dug her fingers into his shoulders, wanting to be anchored, yet needing to let go. She wanted to fly into pleasures that were both terrifying and infinitely tempting.

"Let it happen, love," Tony whispered hoarsely. "Let it happen. Let go."

And she did. For the first time in her life, she let go. She lost herself in the sensations and feelings, and felt as if she were literally being absorbed into Tony, as if she were under his skin, becoming a part of him. She went higher and higher, and Tony was there, holding her, loving her. As she soared into fragmented slivers of ecstasy, she had one solid thought through the mists of sensation. She wasn't alone. Tony was with her.

A rolling rumble of thunder vibrated outside the walls of the stables, and Mallory stirred. Sometime after she'd fallen asleep, Tony had found another blanket and put it over them. Warmth was everywhere, and Mallory had never felt so peaceful or satisfied. She shifted and felt Tony against her back, his arm around her waist, his hand resting near her breasts. His leg, heavy across her thighs, was a welcome weight.

She lay very still, listening to his even breathing, trying to absorb the wonder of what had happened. She'd never experienced anything like it. A completeness that had eluded her for what seemed forever, had finally become a reality. Tears pricked the back of her eyes, and she had to swallow hard.

When she fumbled for his hand and pulled it tightly to her chest, Tony stirred. His fingers laced with hers, and she closed her eyes tightly as he whispered, "Are you awake?"

She tugged his hand up to press her lips to its heat. "Yes."

His lips touched her exposed neck, and when she trembled, he moved even closer to her. His heat was along the length of her back. "Are you cold?"

"No," she whispered, and she shifted until she was facing him on the saddle blankets. The lantern glow was dim and the shadows deep, but she saw every plane and angle with aching clarity. She loved him. It was simple and she accepted it. She touched his chin with a trembling hand, the contact startling in its intensity. Love. It was so unfathomable to her. She didn't understand it—how it could happen so quickly with a man who didn't even really know her.

A crashing bolt of lightning made the air crackle and the tiny windows over the hay light up like it was daytime. In a flashing second, she saw the man beside her, and the idea that the truth could rob her of all this made her stomach knot. Would he still be here if he knew she wasn't Saxon's daughter? That she had no power over the businesses he wanted so badly to control?

The thought was sobering, bringing cold with it that centered within her.

"Tony." She touched her tongue to her lips. "We have to—"

Thunder rolled through the stormy night, and Tony touched her lips with one finger. "In the morning," he whispered. "Everything will work out in the morning."

She closed her eyes for a long moment, then opened them to find Tony just a breath away. That was enough for now. Later, in the morning, she'd face whatever happened. But for now, this was enough. She kissed his finger. "Yes, it will," she managed around the tightness in her throat. One way or another, this would be settled then.

She put her leg over Tony's thigh and skimmed her hand over his shoulder, then under the blanket to press her palm to his middle. When her hand moved lower, she felt the evidence of a desire that was growing in him as quickly as it was in her. He breathed her name on a low moan, then drew her to him, covering her mouth with his as he maneuvered her over him.

Desire that had been sated earlier was back with a force that defied reason. She wanted Tony even more, and as she sat astride him and eased down on him, she let the tears come. He filled her completely and his hands spanned her waist. Her hair falling forward, she looked down at him, memorizing every feature and branding every sensation into her soul.

In the morning, she didn't know what she would have, but for now, she had everything. As she braced her hands on the blanket by his shoulders, she began to move. Then his hands were helping her, matching her rhythm until the need to let go was a living, vital thing. Instinctively Tony seemed to understand, and the pace picked up until his possession of her became as compelling as life itself.

When Mallory knew she was about to explode with joy, Tony thrust deeply, and as they both cried out, the world stopped. The center of the universe was that moment, that tiny room in the stables, and Tony.

*The Watcher stared at the empty bed, anger burning deep and hard. This wasn't the way it was supposed to happen. If she just ran, there wouldn't be an end. And there had to be an end for this to work.*

*A quick look around the room showed that her clothes and personal things were still here. She could be found. She was still close by. Since the roads were closed, her car still stuck in the mud miles from here, and she hadn't taken anything. She was still within reach.*

*Then the idea formed and a seldom-used smile came with it. She was gone. Disappeared. A druggie. Someone who could be there one minute and gone the next. This could be as effective as an accident. Turning, the Watcher moved away into the shadows to go and find Mallory. Then she'd disappear forever.*

Mallory came out of a place of peace and comfort, and the instant she stirred, she remembered. In the next heartbeat, she felt Tony at her back, their bodies aligned perfectly. She slowly opened her eyes, almost not wanting to face the reality of the day as she saw gray light filtering in through the tiny windows at the top of the wall. The lantern had burned out during the night.

She didn't move, afraid if she did, Tony would wake. Right now she just wanted to absorb the feeling of him against her, memories being stored in a secret place in her heart to give her strength to do what she had to do.

There were no choices for her. She knew what she had to do, and she had to do it before she faced Tony again. Carefully she eased away from him, felt his hand slip from her waist, then she was free. But that freedom came at a price of stunning loss when she no longer felt his heat. As quietly as possible, Mallory slipped out from under the blanket and scooted forward to stand on the stone floor.

Rain beat on the roof, and cold, damp air brushed her naked skin. She was shivering when she reached for her clothes and dressed quickly, not looking at Tony. She had to get things settled with Saxon—one way or another. Then she could find Tony and tell him the truth.

As she slipped on her shoes, she knew the chances she was taking. If Tony was only here because he thought she was Saxon's heir, this was all she would ever have. It would be over before it even began, and she would be left with only memories. But she had to take the chance that it was all as real for him as it was for her, that he could forgive her for the lies and that he would understand.

Tony stirred, and Mallory braced herself as she turned to look down at him. She saw him throw one hand over his head onto the hay, but his eyes were closed and his breathing even. Dropping to her haunches, she stayed by him for as long as she dared, just looking at him.

She memorized every detail, the dark lashes against tanned skin, the line of his beard-darkened jaw, the heavy pulse at the hollow of his jaw. For a moment she could almost taste him on her lips, and her hands shook with the need to reach out and brush his dark hair back from his temples. She closed her hands into fists and her nails bit into her palms.

No, she couldn't touch him again. She knew if she did, she wouldn't leave. The world be damned. She wanted to stay here forever, pulling the past night around them like a cloak that could protect them from reality, but that couldn't happen.

Fairy tales and wishes worked in the still of night where the shadows lingered, but not in the light of day. Slowly, she stood and turned from him, and the sense of isolation in her was overwhelming. She tiptoed to the door, eased it back without making any noise and, not trusting herself to look back at the sleeping man, she slipped out into the aisle.

She closed the door and then walked past the stables. And a thought that wouldn't be ignored prodded at her, making her walk faster. What would happen when the role-playing was over and the truth was out? Finally she reached the outer doors and eased one back. Outside it was gray, and the rain had settled into a steady downpour.

She forced herself to plunge out, breaking into a run as she headed toward the house. By the time she got to the shelter of the back entrance, she was soaked and cold. She went inside, and when she reached her room without seeing anyone, she was almost relieved.

She closed the door, feeling the warmth of a freshly laid fire, and inhaled air scented with the sweetness of woodsmoke. The drapes had been opened, letting a gray light filter into the room, and unlit candles had been set on either nightstand.

She had intended to get the note, then go find Saxon, but she didn't have to go to the bed to know the note was gone. The bed had been made, and the darkness of the spread was unrelieved by the ivory paper. And when she scanned the room, she couldn't see it. Someone had it. Maybe Saxon had retrieved it after she'd gone.

She bypassed the bed and headed for the bathroom. As she got to the doorway, she heard something behind her, and she turned just in time to see a folded sheet of paper shoot under the door. She crossed the room to pick up the paper, which was different from that which the first note had been written on. When she opened it, she saw scrawled black handwriting, instead of the block letters of the threat.

*"You're in danger. Lock the door and stay in your room until I come back. Don't open up for anyone. Trust me. Tony."*

She fumbled with the bolt and opened the door, but when she looked out, the hallway was deserted. She thought of going after Tony, but the words of his note stopped her. *"You're in danger."* Saxon was mad, mixing her up with Kate, and she had no idea what he intended to do. She stepped back into the room, closed the door and pushed the safety bolt into place.

She looked down at the note in her hand, staring at the words until they blurred. Why hadn't he knocked on the door? *"Trust me."* She knew right then that she did trust Tony. It was that simple. As she folded the note, she decided to do as he asked.

As cold water trickled down between her shoulder blades, she began to shake, and she knew the first thing she had to do was to get dry and warm. Then she would think of what to do next.

In the marble and gold-plated bathroom, she stripped off her wet clothes, and a tenderness in her breasts brought the night back full force. She'd wait for Tony to come back for her, then she could tell him the truth.

But until then, she dressed in her oversize T-shirt and reached for a towel. She went back into the warm bedroom as she toweled her hair, but as she turned toward the bed, she caught a movement out of the corner of her eye. Tony had come back for her. She turned, saw movement right beside her, then felt something strike her head with such force that she fell sideways.

As the pain exploded through her, she cried out, and the world was gone as she fell into a black void.


"She can't just disappear," Tony muttered as he paced the floor in Saxon's suite. It had been two hours since he'd wakened to find Mallory gone, then hurried to the house and up to her room. It had been empty, every trace of her removed, and no one had seen her.

Saxon sat silently in one of the chairs by the fireplace, with Joyce across from him, her emerald green dress a deep splash of color against the leather. Gene was behind her, his hands pressed to the chair back, and Lawrence stood by the windows, staring out at the gathering night.

As Myra moved silently into the room, carrying a tray of coffee, Tony stopped by Saxon and looked down at the white-haired man. "Saxon, where is she?"

When William put more logs on the fire, Myra laid the tray on the table by Saxon and, without a word, poured his coffee, then nudged it toward him. He waved it aside as he looked up at Tony.

"I wish I knew," he murmured.

"She's on some binge celebrating Christmas and her falling into tons of money," Lawrence said, and Tony glared at the man, killing the urge to beat his face in.

"She's not on drugs."

Lawrence spread his hands with a shrug. "Sure, and I suppose she has some medical condition that makes her pass out and fall down stairs."

Tony met Lawrence's gaze. "She might have been drugged, but she didn't take it by choice."

"What's that supposed to mean?" Joyce asked in her annoying tone.

Tony raked his fingers through his hair. "Someone's been trying to get Mallory out of here."

Lawrence leaned back against the window frame and crossed his arms on his chest. "How about you? You want her to disappear, don't you?"

He stared at the man. At one point he had wanted her to disappear, but now he just wanted her safe. "I'm not happy with some long-lost daughter suddenly surfacing when Saxon's redoing his will, but there's a big difference with wanting to harm her."

"Oh, you think we're up to no good, that we're plotting against her?"

Tony knew it sounded irrational, but that's exactly what he thought. "Are you?"

Lawrence moved abruptly to the bar near Saxon's desk. "That's *your* family's style, not mine," he muttered as he poured himself a hefty serving of whiskey.

Saxon cut in. "That's enough. We're here to figure out what to do."

Tony looked back at Saxon, shocked to see tension and a tinge of paleness in the man's face. Could he actually care about Mallory? Was there a thread of humanity in the man? It had been easier for Tony to deal with him when Saxon was heartless. "What are we going to do?"

Saxon brushed a hand over his face. "I don't know. We've looked everywhere we can think to look. All I can figure is she took off walking. I'll send William down to where her car is and see if she's been there."

Joyce shifted in the seat, her rigid posture getting even stiffer. "Uncle Saxon, it's Christmas. Do we just put all of our plans on hold because someone who is obviously a drug addict—" she glared at Tony, daring him to say something "—goes off to do God knows what?"

Saxon scowled at Joyce. "There is no celebration while my daughter's missing."

Joyce bit her lip but knew better than to challenge the old man. Tony couldn't just stay in this room waiting for something to happen. He headed for the door. "I'm going back down to the stables and that area to look around." He looked back. "William, are you going to go to her car?"

William looked at Saxon. "If the mister wants me to."

"I do," Saxon murmured. "Tony?"

"Yes?"

"What did she say to you when you saw her the last time?"

He hesitated, then spoke the truth. "That she was worried you were confusing her with her mother."

He didn't expect Saxon to almost shrink in front of his eyes. The man sat back, his hands clasped in front of him, and his skin drawn looking.

The bark of laughter from Lawrence intruded. "Then why in the hell did she come here?"

"To find her family," Tony said. "And look what she found. Fools—and worse yet, people who hated her for just existing."

Lawrence put down his drink on the surface of the bar with a cracking sound, then strode across to where Tony stood by the door. "Who do you think you are? Simon Pure? God knows what you'd do to someone who got in your way! Maybe *you* took care of her, the way your father *took care* of people who annoyed him."

Tony barely stopped himself from striking Lawrence, but the desire burned in him. And he wondered just how much of his father he actually had in him. The idea of putting a bullet in this man wasn't farfetched at the moment. "If you believe that, you'd better watch your back. You're way past annoying me." He paused then, adding, "Larry."

He heard Joyce gasp as Lawrence leaned close to Tony. "You son of a—"

"Lawrence, shut up!" Lawrence jerked around at Saxon's loud command, and Saxon stood. For a moment he was unsteady, then he pulled himself straight, drawing composure around himself like a cloak. "Just get out." He looked at Joyce and Gene. "All of you. If you aren't going to help, leave."

Joyce stood, and with Gene in tow, headed for the door. They brushed past Tony without a glance, and left. Lawrence was furious, but he muttered, "Merry Christmas," and pushed past Tony.

Tony stood back and looked at Saxon. The man nodded to Myra and William. "The car, William. And Myra, check out the north wing where it's closed."

Myra nodded and left with William following her. When everyone was gone, Tony said, "How seriously are you taking this father thing?"

The old man met Tony's gaze with his deep blue eyes. "She's the most important thing to me right now. I have to find her."

Tony could have echoed those very words and known he'd spoken the truth. Mallory had come into his world and absorbed every part of it. The memory of sleeping next to her, of waking in the night and feeling her against him, had burned into his mind, as surely as had the feeling of her under him.

He'd never been blindsided by a woman like this before in his life. He'd never felt as if his feet could be knocked out from under him, and his breath driven from his body, just by a touch. He'd been safe from feelings until now. And now he didn't want to be safe. He just wanted to see her and make sense out of what had happened between them.

She couldn't just disappear, not when he'd finally figured out what it meant to be connected to another human being. That almost brought laughter from him. Forty years and he'd finally figured out the secret to life. He sobered. He just hoped he wasn't too late.

"We'll find her, Saxon," he said, and left, closing the door behind him. He had to find her.

Christmas music surrounded Mallory, and the scent of pine was everywhere.

She was warm and happy, sitting by a huge tree with twinkling lights and red and green glass ornaments. Presents were piled under the tree, and a happiness that defied description filled her.

It was the Christmas she'd never had. The Christmas she'd dreamed of all the years she'd been alone and had tried to ignore the holidays. Then she knew why it was special. Tony was there, coming toward her, his arms held out, his face smiling. And she knew that everything she'd been looking for all her life was here with her.

She felt her heart leap at the sight, and she held out her own hands, needing to touch him, wanting to feel him. But as he got closer, someone was with him. Saxon came out of the shadows, his face distorted, and when she looked to Tony, he'd stopped. He stared at her. The connection gone.

Someone had her by the wrists, and the music changed into a cacophony of shrill sounds as she cried out for Tony to help her. But he didn't move. "You're a liar," he gritted. "A liar." He turned from her, melting into shadows.

She tried to cry out, but something was on her mouth, something killing her words before they even formed, and suddenly she was awake. The nightmare dissolved, but as she regained consciousness, she fell into another nightmare, one she couldn't waken from.

There was blackness everywhere. Her head pounded, and her wrists and ankles were bound. She was lying on her side on something hard and abrasive, and rough cloth gagged her mouth. The perpetual Christmas music was off in the distance, and the smell of dank, stale air assailed her nostrils.

She was tied so tightly she could barely feel her hands and feet, and raw fear made her heart pound in her chest. As her head throbbed in unison with her heart, she tried to remember, to figure out what was going on.

She'd been in her room, alone. Then someone was there—Tony. She thought it had been Tony, but she couldn't remember. Just a blow to her head, then pain and nothing.

Tony. She swallowed, trying to ease the tight dryness in her mouth, and the ache of helpless tears burned her eyes. She'd let down her guard for the first time in a long time, and she'd let herself fall in love. *Love.* She didn't even know if she knew what love was. She shifted, felt the ties at her wrist bite into her skin, and tears slipped from her eyes.

# CHAPTER THIRTEEN

But the tears weren't the soft tears of wonder they'd been during the night with Tony. They came with racking sobs and an ache in her soul that defied description. Mallory was as mad as Saxon, every bit as crazy. Breathless, she forced herself to stop crying. She couldn't breathe and she couldn't do anything until she figured out what was happening.

She could barely make out the shadows of a low-ceilinged room that seemed to have stone walls. The air was closed and musty, with no windows and no light. A dungeon. She knew that no one knew where she was. She hadn't seen anyone, and Tony was the only one she'd had contact with. He was the only person who knew she had been in her room. *"Don't open up for anyone. Trust me. Tony."*

She could barely absorb it. Trust him. She had. She'd wanted to so badly. Pure madness. She struggled against the confines of the ropes that bound her wrists and ankles. She wasn't going to wait here, to face whatever he had in mind for her. The rope bit into her skin, but the physical pain was nothing compared to the emotional pain she was experiencing. She was on her own again, alone, and her survival was up to her.

The muffled Christmas music was driving her mad, and as she twisted back, she felt her feet strike something hard. Cautiously, she wiggled her body backward until she felt something rough and cold and damp. The wall. With her fingers, she felt a sharp edge of stone. She twisted until her hands were against the stone, and slowly she began to rub the ropes up and down on the surface.

Her shoulders ached horribly and her hands were almost numb, but she kept going. And just when she was certain it was all futile, she felt something pop. She tugged at the ropes, but they didn't give. Frantically, she rubbed against the stone again, over and over, ignoring the nicks to her skin, and the radiating pain in her arms and shoulders. Then something popped again, and this time she felt a degree of slackness in the ties.

She inhaled as deeply as she could through her nose, then, bracing herself, she jerked her hands as hard as she could. Fiery pain burned her skin, but at the last minute, the rope gave way and her hands were free. She lay there for a long moment, just getting her breath and dealing with the pain in her wrists, then she struggled to a sitting position and rubbed her hands together. The tingling was almost unbearable, but if she was free, she could deal with it.

When she tried to tug the gag from her mouth, her hands refused to cooperate. They felt thick and awkward, her fingers were almost numb. She shook them hard, then rubbed them back and forth on her bare legs, frustration all but choking her. Then she felt the tingling in her hands change to a throbbing ache, and she could flex her fingers.

Clumsily she hooked her forefinger in the side of the gag and felt her nail scrape her cheek. But she didn't stop. She got a grip on the cloth and pulled on it until it slid down around her neck, and she took gasping breaths that almost made her dizzy.

She quickly pulled her knees to her chest and reached for the bindings on her ankles. It seemed an eternity before she could make her fingers work accurately enough to undo the knots in the heavy rope, but when she was finally free, she sank back against the wall. Cautiously she touched the spot above her right ear where the pain seemed to center.

She almost gasped at the tenderness. Gingerly she prodded at it and felt a swelling under her scalp. Her hair felt sticky, and she knew she'd bled. She exhaled, trying to think.

She had to figure out where she was, and then do whatever it took to get out. Once she was free, she was going to run and keep running until she was so far from this place and these people that they'd become a distant, horrible memory.

She crossed her legs and rubbed at her ankles and bare feet, massaging with her aching fingers to try to get her circulation going again. She didn't need to see to know that her ankles were raw—the skin was sensitive where her fingers touched it. Finally her feet began to throb, and as they settled into an uncomfortable aching, Mallory used the wall for support and tried to stand.

At first she fell back to the blanket, then finally managed to get to her feet and stand. With her free hand, she reached out in front of her, but felt nothing. Then above her, and her fingers skimmed the wood of the ceiling. She kept contact with the wall behind her, stumbling along the cold stone floor until she hit a wall.

She groped in front of her, then felt something like metal. She fingered it. A metal bar, then another one not more than two inches from it, and another and another. A gate of some sort. She felt a handle and pulled on it. There was no sound when the gate swung back toward her. The hinges were well oiled.

Mallory hesitated, then felt in front of her with her foot. The floor there was the same—smooth cold stone. Holding her hands out, she went forward carefully, and after two steps, she felt a wall of rough wood. She felt to her left and touched a wall, then to her right, but there was nothing there. This wasn't a closet.

She took hesitant steps to the right, keeping one hand out in front of her, the other on the wall to keep her oriented. The music seemed to follow her, faint but persistent. Then the wall curved, and Mallory's foot struck something. She bent down, sweeping her hands out in front of her to figure out what it was. Then she knew she'd found wooden stairs. Straightening, she felt for the wall again, and took the step, then another and another, until she'd gone up about ten and come to a landing.

She realized the music was getting louder, and her eyes were adjusting to the tiny bit of light that was there, enough for her to make out a tunnel or passageway. As she went forward, she saw a glow starting to penetrate the darkness.

She knew she'd found a way out. Adrenaline surged through her. She went as fast as she could in the nar-

row corridor, but when she got close to the light, her
hopes were dashed. There wasn't a door, just a panel
about eye level that was no bigger than a heating grate.

She went closer and looked through an ornate metal
grillwork and realized she was looking into the library lit by candlelight. The music was louder here,
about the same volume as the music had been in the
dining room before, and playing for no one.

She could see the open doors to the room, the
bookshelves and the table by the curtained windows.
The opening had to be near the shelves where the stone
wall had wood paneling, right by the door. She ran her
fingers over the wall, felt the seam of a low door, but
couldn't find any way to open it. She tried to move the
grille, but it wouldn't give. Then she realized it
wouldn't do her any good, anyway. She couldn't yell
for help. Anyone might hear her, including Tony.

Mallory drew back, the idea of seeing Tony again as
frightening as the idea of being bound and gagged in
the dungeon. She looked to her left, saw that the corridor kept going, and she moved away from the light.
She headed down the corridor, rounded a corner and
saw another light source.

This time she looked into the kitchen. It was empty,
but coffee was going in the coffeemaker, and the rem-
nants of sandwiches were on a tray nearby. The door
here didn't have a handle, either, and even the hinges
were set into the wood where they couldn't be tam-
pered with.

There had to be a way out of here. She could tell it
had been used—the hinges on the lower door were
kept oiled for some reason, and the corridor would
have been thick with dust if the passages hadn't been

used. So there had to be a secret to opening. But she couldn't figure it out.

She knew this house wasn't haunted. Someone had been watching and waiting. The sense of being under scrutiny all the time hadn't just been her imagination. Someone moved through these corridors and peered into the rooms at will.

She turned and kept going. Now the light was good enough for her to make out the stairs before she came to them. A thin railing had been tacked into the stone on the right, and she gripped it and went up. At the top, she knew she was on the second floor. She moved toward another doorway, looked through the grating and saw an empty bedroom, but she could tell it belonged to Joyce and Gene. The horrible ruby red dress Joyce had worn the first night was hanging on the back of the armoire door.

Mallory tried to open that door, but couldn't find a way. She knew there had to be some trick to opening the panels, but she kept going. Sooner or later, she'd have to find some exit. The next part of the corridor was long and darker, making Mallory use her hands for direction again, until she turned another corner and saw light.

She headed for it, and when she looked through the grille, she was shocked to find herself looking into her bathroom. No wonder she'd felt vulnerable. She had a clear view of the tub and shower, and into the bedroom. There was something covering the grille here—then she realized it had to be one of the mirrors. She could see through it, but from the other side, it was just a mirror.

She shivered. No wonder Saxon had told her not to talk out of character anywhere except his room. He knew all about this and knew others could be in here at any given time. The wall curved, following the shape of the tower with irregular stones jutting into the corridor, forcing the path out and around the barriers. But the peephole was right there, and when she looked through it, she saw her own room. The hole was to one side of the fireplace, probably in the wood panel with the horse carved into it. And she'd never noticed it.

She could see the bed clearly in the flickering of candlelight as she felt along the seams of the door, frantically searching for any way to make it open. But there was nothing. Frustration choked her. She was so close. If she could just get in there and get her things, she could escape, but there was no way to get the door open. She felt tears choking her. She had to get out. She had to.

Frustration drove her to kick at the door, and she was shocked when she heard a faint click. The door, maybe four feet high, swung silently back. She stepped through it into her room. The air seemed fresh in here, and warmth came from a fire that someone had stoked recently.

The idea of being watched made her stomach sick, and not knowing by whom was even more disturbing. She quickly crossed to the armoire to get fresh clothes so she could get out of the soiled nightshirt, but when she opened the door, it was empty. Everything—even the evening gowns Saxon had bought for her—was gone.

She pulled the drawers open, one after the other, but they were empty. She turned and looked around the room. She had nothing in here. No clothes, not even her purse or the luggage that had been stacked to one side of the door. Someone had cleaned out every last trace of her. It was as if she had never existed. But she did exist. And she wasn't going to let anything end here except her stupidity in taking the job and trusting Tony.

She stood in the middle of the room, her mind racing. Then she knew what she could do. She remembered the clothes in the stables, some jeans and shirts, even some boots pushed against the wall. And the horses were there. The idea of riding a horse out was a possibility, if it came down to that. But just the clothes would help. All she needed to do was to get to the stables unseen. From there she could do whatever it took to survive.

She hurried toward the door, but before she could reach for it, it opened. When she saw Tony in front of her, his hair damp, and his clothes darkened at the shoulders with water, she felt as if the world had screeched to a halt. His face was stamped with shock, the same shock she knew was in her expression. And before she could react, he was in the room, rushing toward her.

She tried to run, but he had her by the wrists, and the pain from her raw skin blazed through her. Bolting into action, she jerked free, and without an alternative, she flew at him with her hands curled into fists. She swung at him, striking his shoulder, and as he tried to grab her hands, she beat on his chest.

"Bastard, bastard, bastard," she sobbed as she struck out in a frenzy of fear and pain.

"Mallory, stop," he said as his hands captured her arms, his strength overwhelming. "Stop."

Mallory looked up at him through the blur of tears and knew she couldn't fight whatever Tony was going to do. But her heart lurched when she saw no anger in his face, no threat, just confusion and pain, then shock when he looked at her wrists. She followed his gaze and saw the skin raw from the effort she'd made to free herself, a set of obscene bracelets as reminders of what she had gone through.

"God," he whispered, then looked back at Mallory, and in the next instant, he pulled her to him.

Slowly she collapsed against him, and as his arms surrounded her, she knew that if she was damned by loving him, so be it. Nothing could change it. Pressing her face into his chest, she felt him rest his chin on her bent head, and he whispered, "What happened? Where were you? Who did this to you?"

She rubbed her head against his chest, unable to utter words that she'd believed were true until a second ago. When she heard more footsteps at the doorway, Mallory closed her eyes tightly, afraid to let go of Tony, yet afraid to hold on.

"You found her, Mr. Carella," Myra said in her precise English.

Mallory looked around Tony's arm and saw the woman coming into the room, toward the two of them. Then, before Mallory knew what was happening, Myra lifted her hand and silver flashed through the air, striking Tony in the back of the head. Mallory heard the sickening impact, then saw Tony stiffen.

His eyes widened, rolled up, and he started to crumple.

Mallory grabbed at his jacket, trying to catch him, but his weight was too much for her, and she found herself slipping to the floor with him. She ended on her knees with Tony laying unconscious in front of her. She held tightly to his damp jacket as she looked up at Myra.

"Wh-why?" she gasped.

"A nuisance," she muttered, motioning to Tony with the barrel of the gun. "Now he has to go, too." She actually smiled. "But this might work out. The two of you leaving . . . together. It should drive a stake through Saxon's heart to have another woman run from him."

Mallory shook her head. "Myra, no, this is crazy. Why are you doing this?"

The woman came closer. "It should have been you the first time."

"What time?"

"With the umbrella, coming out of the theater. I thought it was you. Then you turned up here."

Mallory's hands tightened on Tony's jacket, raw fear making her feel sick. Sara had been almost killed because Myra thought she was Mallory. She stared up at Myra, looking into the eyes of cool madness.

"Did you think you could just walk in here and ruin everything like your mother did?" The woman pressed her free hand to her chest. "Saxon wanted me . . . until your mother came along. Then I was nothing. I wasn't even good enough to be in his bed again. But I made sure Kate was not in it, either." She waved the gun in an arch through the air. "The stupid woman," she all but spat. "It was almost too easy to make Saxon think she'd been teasing other men. The woman flirted all the time. And Saxon hated Kate for that."

Mallory felt Tony stir, but Myra didn't seem to notice. She was lost in the past, in a world of hate. "Saxon let me stay, but as his housekeeper. He never looked at me again, but I knew that sooner or later, he would realize how stupid he had been about Kate. Sooner or later."

"Myra, that's all past. It's over."

"Over?" Her eyes widened. "It is not over as long as you are around. He would have never even known about you, if Henry Welting had not been digging into the past. I knew about you, but I never knew that anyone else could find out."

Mallory shook her head. "You knew?"

"Of course. I knew there was a child. Unlike Saxon, I knew where Kate went. She had talked about the city often enough, and about a friend she had. She was there when I found her months later. You had just been born."

"Kate had a child?"

Myra looked confused by the question. "Of course."

"Myra, listen to me. I'm not Saxon's child. I never even knew him until a few days ago when Henry Welting contacted me at the theater to play the part of his daughter."

She shook her head. "He found you and brought you here."

"No—I mean, yes, he did, but I'm not Kate's child. I'm an actress. Saxon's paying me to do this."

Myra came closer to Mallory and suddenly laughed, a shattering sound in the room. "I know Kate's daughter when I see her. You're the image of that woman."

"I'm not Kate's daughter. My mother's name wasn't even Kate."

Myra sobered. "Kate wasn't her real name. That was just Saxon's pet name for her, you know, after Kate in *The Taming of the Shrew*. They fought so hard sometimes, and Saxon used to tell me she was his Kate. Her real name was Mary Carpenter."

The declaration stunned Mallory. Mary Carpenter. Her mother's name. She felt Tony stir, but she couldn't look away from Myra. "Are you...you sure that was her name?"

"Of course I am. She has haunted me for years. I would never forget that name."

Mallory closed her eyes for a moment, sickness rising in her throat. Could Saxon do that? Could he bring her here without telling her the truth? Why would he? And she knew the answer to that with a certainty that only increased her nausea. He wanted to use her and see if she might be worth keeping. Tony had been horribly accurate when he told her that Saxon used and discarded people that didn't measure up.

The cruel twist left her numb, unable to fully comprehend the fact that she had found her father. Or her father had found her. A man her mother had turned her back on and never returned to. A man who was cruel and hard and mean enough to play a game with his own child.

Everyone in this house had been dealing with the truth, while she'd lived a lie. Mallory was startled by Myra jabbing her in the shoulder with the barrel of the gun. When she looked up, the woman said, "Come on. Get up."

She looked down at Tony and knew she wasn't going anywhere with the woman. "No."

Myra struck Mallory in the shoulder this time, the pain sharp and cutting. "I said get up. We do not have a lot of time before the others come up here."

She slowly eased Tony onto the floor, wincing at the blood that trickled down his temple to his jaw. With trembling hands, she smoothed his hair, hating the stillness of his form. Then she started to get to her feet, and she knew it was all up to her if she wanted Tony and herself to survive this madness.

As she straightened, the shrill sound of a telephone ringing startled her. And it startled Myra. The woman turned toward the noise, and Mallory knew this was probably the only chance she would have. She lunged at Myra as the woman started to turn back toward her, and she heard a scream, then the rushing of air. The next thing she knew, she was falling, tangled with Myra, and the hardness of the gun was at her stomach, caught between her body and the housekeeper's.

"No!" Myra's scream barely died out when the sound of the gun going off shattered the room.

If time could freeze, Mallory knew it had at that moment. An eternity could have passed before she could move, and she rolled to one side onto the floor and away from Myra. The acrid odor of gunpowder burned her nose and throat. Then she felt heat at her middle and looked down at her stomach. Brilliant red stained the white of her nightshirt, and when she pressed her hand to it, she felt warmth and stickiness. Blood.

Her head spun and nausea choked her. Then someone was over her, grabbing her by her arm and lifting her up. The next moment she was in Tony's arms, his ragged breathing in her ear. "I...I'm shot," she breathed, staring at the blood on the hand she held in front of her face.

"No, you aren't. Myra is," Tony said as he carried her to the bed.

She heard William yelling, his words a blur of sound and anger, but she didn't have the strength to focus on them. As Tony sat her on the bed, others came into the room, and sounds of shock and urgency were everywhere, but all she could focus on was Tony dropping to his haunches in front of her.

He touched her bloody hand where it lay limply on her knee. "It's not your blood," he said. "It's not. You're all right."

She looked into his face and at the blood staining his temple. "You're bleeding."

"I'm alive, and so are you."

Voices seemed to be everywhere, but Mallory couldn't focus past Tony, past his hold on her hand or the fact that they were both very much alive. They'd survived. But what was left?

"Mallory." She heard Saxon say her name, and as Tony let go of her hand and moved to one side, she saw the older man in front of her. The bloodred of his robe made his skin look ashen, and his expression was pinched. As she looked up at him, she realized he looked very old.

A shocking combination of anger and uncertainty mingled in her, yet she didn't have an idea what she felt about him . . . about her father. Her father. The words held no reality for her, and there was no one emotion she could grab a hold on. She could hate this man for his vicious manipulations, yet there was a wonder in finally facing the only blood relation she had in this world.

"Are you hurt?" he asked in a shaky voice.

Hurt? She felt fragmented, as if she had no identity at all. When Tony moved closer and touched her shoulder, she didn't let herself hold on to him. He was as much a mystery to her as this man in front of her. She tugged at the front of her nightshirt, hating the feeling of the now cold blood sticking to her skin. "No . . . I'll survive," she whispered.

He grimaced and she knew he saw her wrists. "Myra?"

She sensed movement to her left and glanced in the direction just in time to see William carrying his mother from the room. She couldn't tell if the woman was dead or alive. "Yes, Myra," she said in a low voice.

"I'm sorry," he said. "I never thought she could do anything like this."

Mallory looked back at Saxon. "How could you do it?"

Saxon turned back to her and seemed to shrink even more, the strong, controlling man she'd met, dissolving right in front of her. "How did you find out?"

She ignored his question. "It's true?"

He pushed his hands in the pockets of his robe, but he didn't hedge. "Yes, it's true."

The impact of his words almost drove the air out of her lungs, and she gripped the edge of the bed tightly to keep sitting upright.

"Henry Welting found you by accident when he was trying to find out about Kate's life before she died. But he found out that Kate was carrying you when she left me. That you're my flesh and blood. I wanted to see you."

"So you got me to come here for a job, to come here in the role of one of your employees." Her voice was starting to shake, and she didn't know if it was from shock or from the anger that was growing in her.

"Employee?" Lawrence's sharp question just past Saxon was jarring, and she knew that Tony was staring at her, but Mallory didn't look away from Saxon.

"What was it, a trial run, trying to see if I was worth keeping? Would you have just paid me off and let me go at the end of the two weeks without telling me, if I didn't measure up?"

Mallory could see a vague trembling in the way Saxon held his head, and his paleness was even more pronounced. "I didn't know then," he whispered, "I swear. But now—"

"Were you willing to use me to weed out the others? My God, you had to know how they hated me, how they wanted me out of here. Myra could have killed me because of your lies!"

"Mallory, please, I...I'm sorry. I was wrong."

As she heard the words, she wondered what it had cost him to be able to say them. Saxon Mills admitting he'd been wrong. It almost made her laugh, but she knew that was the hysteria and shock. "Dead wrong, Saxon."

"I know. And now that you're here, I want you to stay. I want my daughter with me. I'm so sorry for the life you had, for the grief Kate had. I never knew. I honestly thought she was in Europe until Henry found out she'd never left the city. I missed the first part of your life, but I want to be there for the rest of my life, for whatever time I have left. That's the truth. That's all I have now, the truth."

# CHAPTER FOURTEEN

Mallory didn't know how to fight his words, but she knew she couldn't stay here. Truth was something that had been absent since she walked through the door with Tony. She didn't know how she felt about Saxon, not any more than she knew why Tony had made love to her, or why he was still here, standing a foot from her, not talking, just watching.

His presence was so overwhelming that she had to make herself not look at him. "I'm leaving as soon as I can."

Saxon shrugged, but didn't try to argue. "I understand. You can leave tomorrow. The phone lines are working. I had Myra bring a phone in here before we knew you had disappeared. Call anyone you like. I'll have you taken wherever you like. But remember what I've said. You're my child, and even though Kate and I never could make things work, I want to make things work with you. I'll do whatever it takes, however long it takes."

Mallory felt her eyes burn, and she had come to hate tears. She hadn't cried for so many years, but in this house the tears had been a constant companion for her. She looked away from Saxon and Tony, and saw Joyce at the foot of the bed, her face pale and her hand holding tightly to the bedpost. Lawrence was near the door, staring at her.

She stood, her legs wobbly, but strong enough to hold her. This is where her mother had been, in the middle of this madness, facing this man, and she'd run. Mallory knew the urge, the sense that if she ran and didn't look back, this could all dissolve and she could be back to normal.

"Get out," she whispered.

"Mallory?"

She heard Tony's voice by her side, but couldn't look at the man. "All of you, get out," she breathed.

She closed her eyes, trying to push away the past, the night her mother had taken off from here and run into a life filled with pain and loneliness. The night she'd run away with Saxon Mills's child. Her mother. The woman who had never told her the truth, just the way her father hadn't until now. The mother whose picture was still in this house, the only picture Mallory had ever seen of her.

She swallowed sickness, then heard the door click shut. When she opened her eyes, the room was empty. She was alone. The way she had been for what seemed like forever—at least, until she'd been with Tony. That memory knotted her middle, and as Mallory turned, she saw the blood on the floor.

She ran for the bathroom, barely making it before she retched over and over again in the toilet. When there was nothing left, she sank back on her heels, one hand gripping the porcelain bowl. Then she fumbled for a towel off of the vanity, and as she pressed the terry cloth to her mouth, she looked up and saw where the peephole from the corridor was hidden behind the mirror.

She struggled to her feet, ignoring her image bouncing back at her. She refused to focus on her pale face, tangled hair, the blood darkening on her white nightshirt, and she reached up until she caught the terry cloth of the towel on the corner of the mirror. She let go, leaving the towel to dangle over the mirror, shutting out any view from the hidden tunnel behind it.

She felt dirty and soiled and sick. Crossing to the shower, she turned on the faucet. While the steamy heat filled the glassed-in cubicle, she stripped off the nightshirt and dropped it in the wicker wastebasket by the door.

Then she went back to the shower, opened the door and stepped under the steamy heat. She felt stinging at her wrists and ankles, then in her hair above her ear, but she stayed under the water, letting its heat wash over her and around her. But no matter how long she stayed under the scalding heat, nothing warmed the coldness in her soul.

Mallory woke from a restless sleep to darkness and the sure knowledge that she was being watched. She sat bolt upright in bed, the air chilly, and she turned to the secret panel with the grating by the fireplace. But the towel she put over it the way she'd covered the one in the bathroom was still in place.

She fumbled to her right, felt the light and pressed the switch. Electricity had been restored before she climbed into bed last night, and now the low light flashed on, but it barely touched the shadows in the room. Mallory glanced around, and she felt her heart catch when she saw Tony to her left. He'd drawn a chair close to the bed, and he was sitting there, watching her, silent.

Mallory tugged the blankets up, horribly conscious of wearing nothing. Her clothes were still gone, and she hadn't found anything to sleep in. "What are you doing here?" she asked.

"Waiting." His voice came through the shadows, deep and soft.

Her hands tightened on the blankets she clutched to her breasts. "I asked you to leave earlier."

"That was hours ago."

She shifted until she felt the cold wood of the head-board at her bare back. She had nothing left to deal with anyone right now, least of all Tony. "What time is it now?"

"Somewhere around three in the morning last time I looked. They took Myra to the hospital. William managed to get one of the cars through the mud-slide area, and he called an hour ago. The woman's in serious condition, but she'll live. Then they'll have to decide what to do."

Mallory didn't want to relive the moment the gun went off. "She's crazy."

"She probably has been for years. She's obsessed with Saxon, and he knew it. He let her be as long as it worked for him. He even put up with William's antics. I don't understand it all, but I guess it boils down to Saxon doing what he wants to do to get what he wants. No matter what."

"No matter what," she echoed, bitterness lingering, but not as strong as it had been hours ago.

"I called about the girl Myra tried to kill at the theater."

"What *about* Sara?"

"She regained consciousness. She's not out of the woods, but she's getting stronger."

"Thank God," she breathed.

"How about you? How are you feeling?"

She shrugged. "I don't know. Numb, confused, angry, sad. Take your pick."

"I can imagine. You've been through the ringer, haven't you?"

"I guess so. Saxon's the great manipulator, isn't he?"

"He always has been, but right now he's beaten, Mallory. I've never seen him this way."

"He's not going to die. You said yourself that he doesn't believe he'll die until he stops working on this house. From the looks of it, he's got another twenty years before they complete the new wing."

"He's alive now, and he's been pacing in his room for hours, waiting, hoping you'd come to see him."

"Why would I want to see him right now?"

"He's your father."

"He's my father biologically, not in any other way."

Tony didn't move, but he didn't stop talking. "He's your father, period. His blood is in your veins, and you're his little piece of immortality. You and your children, and your children's children."

"Stop it," she muttered, not wanting to hear him wax philosophical, especially not about any future she could have.

"I've realized something tonight—a Christmas gift of sorts, I guess. And it's pretty monumental."

"I don't want to—"

"I was wrong," he said bluntly.

"What about?"

"My father. I didn't have to like what he was or what he did. I didn't have to have any part in it, but he was still my father. I should never have turned my back on him completely."

She closed her eyes tightly, hating the way she could sense the pain and regret in Tony's words. "It's the past. It's over," she whispered.

"Exactly. It's the past. It's over and done. And it can't be changed."

She opened her eyes and looked at Tony, a man almost lost in the shadows. Almost, but not quite. She could see his hands gripping the arms of the leather chair, and his eyes, dark shadows turned in her direction. "Then why are you telling me all this?"

"Because it's not too late for you. Don't walk out on Saxon. Have whatever relationship you can have, no matter how limited, but don't turn your back on him."

She stared at Tony. "I thought you hated him."

"No, I never hated him. Maybe I didn't like him, but hate...no."

"You want me to stay here?"

"I want you to stay in Saxon's life, for your sake as much as for his."

"But I thought you wanted me out of here. You offered me a hundred thousand dollars to leave."

"That was before."

"Before what?" she asked, not at all certain she really wanted to know.

"Before I understood what loving someone meant."

Her throat tightened at the sound of the word *love*. "I hardly think what Saxon feels is love," she muttered.

"I think he does love you...in his own way. But I wasn't talking about Saxon." He stood and came to the bed. "I was talking about me."

"I don't understand."

"I'm in love, real love. You know, the kind where you honestly forget about yourself and only want the best for the person you care about?"

She barely stopped herself from covering her ears to block out words that cut at her. She couldn't bear to hear him speak of love, and she forced herself to say words that would stop it all before the pain got too great. "Tony, stop. I have to tell you what I've decided."

"What is it?"

"Before I fell asleep, I had a long time to think and sort through things. I accepted the fact that Saxon is my father, good or bad, and I'll try and have a relationship with him. It might be very limited, but I'll have something with him. But I won't take a thing from him—not money or stocks or anything.

"I'll probably be waiting tables and acting in little theaters all my life, and I'll be scraping by. Joyce and Lawrence are welcome to Saxon's money and businesses. I don't want anything from the man, except to have him as a father. So you're too late. I don't have a thing you want. I never will have."

She was stunned when he actually smiled down at her. "I don't think that's entirely true."

"What isn't?"

He sat on the side of the bed, making the mattress shift with his weight. "As for you being poor, I'd be willing to bet a hundred thousand dollars that you're going to make a fortune on the stage. Your performance since you got here has been stunning. You had me fooled, and everyone else in the house." His smile faltered. "As far as you not having what I want, I'm sorry, you're wrong. You're all I want."

She pressed back against the headboard, the cold air in the room making her start to shake. "No, don't."

"Mallory, all I want from you is you. I don't give a damn if you're Saxon's daughter or a waitress in a coffee shop. I just want you."

"But you've been trying to get rid of me ever since we met."

"I know. At first I was trying to get you out of here because I thought you were a Mills, and a Mills takes what they want, no matter who suffers. I thought you were a clone of Lawrence and Joyce, going for the gold, and to hell with the consequences."

"So when you couldn't buy me off, you decided to try and charm me into falling in love with you?" The words were bitter on her tongue, but had to be said.

"No, never that. *You* charmed me. I found a gentleness in you, a vulnerability and uniqueness I'd never dealt with before in my life." She heard him take a shaky breath. "Most of all, you made me fall in love with you."

The words hung between them, and Mallory couldn't begin to take them in. "Tony, don't."

He actually chuckled, a rueful sound. "Can you believe it? I fell in love with the daughter of Saxon Mills. The man is soulless, as far as I'm concerned, yet he'd produced this person who is exquisite, and a person who touched me on so many levels that I still can't comprehend it all."

She wondered if she was hallucinating, that her desperation to have someone love her totally and completely was producing this moment when it seemed she could have everything. If she just reached out for it. "But... but I told you, I won't take anything from Saxon. I mean it, Tony, I really do."

"I know you do, love, and it's all right."

"But you..." She had made up fairy tales all her life, but nothing compared to this. "You want control of the businesses. You said so."

"Of course I do. But if I don't get it, it's not the end of the world. I've got enough of my own interests to keep me busy for a long time. I just hate to see something that could be great, ruined by the stupidity of the controlling parties." He shifted, coming closer to her. "I've done enough of that during my life. But it ends right here."

"How?" she whispered, needing desperately to know.

When he touched her, she didn't move. When his fingers closed over her bare shoulders, she barely breathed. "By telling you that I love you, and if you'll let me, I want to love you for the rest of our lives."

"Do you really mean that?"

His fingers moved on her skin, caressing it and sending shivers of delight through her body. "More than anything I've ever said before." His touch stilled, and she saw uncertainty in his eyes. "Say you love me, that you want to be with me."

She swallowed hard before she could speak. "Love you? I love you so much," she whispered, and the sheet slipped from her fingers.

Tony pulled her to him, and she buried her face in his chest. She wrapped her arms around his waist, holding tightly to him, not about to let reality slip away from her this time.

"That's all I need to know," he whispered just before his lips found hers.

Mallory lost herself in the caress, and the next thing she knew, Tony was with her in the bed, the urgency of his need for her echoed in her own needs. Time didn't exist, and as she went to him, offering herself with an abandon she'd never known in her life, she felt as if she'd come home. Really home. She belonged in a way she never had, and it had nothing to do with a place, nothing to do with anything but Tony.

For the first time in her life, she knew she had a future. And it was in her arms. As Tony explored her with his hands, and his mouth ravished her, Mallory arched to him, and when he came to her, filling her and showing her how much he loved her, she knew that reality was as thrilling as any dream she'd ever managed to dream.

"I love you," Tony whispered hoarsely. "Marry me?"

When he was over her, she looked up into his face. As sensations built on sensations, Mallory whispered, "Yes, oh, yes," and in that moment everything turned into shimmering ecstasy, and the world became a place of joy and happiness. She had her family.

*   *   *

### January 1

New Year's Day was sunny and warm, a perfect day for a wedding.

The hastily arranged ceremony had taken place in Saxon's suite, the room transformed with roses everywhere and sunlight that had flooded in through the windows.

When Mallory had turned to Tony at the conclusion of the vows, she'd felt her heart catch in her chest. The sight of him brought happiness that knew no bounds, and when they'd kissed, it was as if their future had been sealed.

She had everything she'd ever dreamed of.

She hurried back to her room to change out of the simple white suit and into clothes for traveling. She didn't know where they were going for a honeymoon, but Tony had arranged it all.

After she undressed and put her dress away in the armoire, she stood very still in the silence. The room had gone from a place where she felt spied on and uncomfortable, to a place of joy the night Tony had told her he loved her and wanted to marry her. The tunnels and secret room were sealed up now, and this place was a welcome haven for her, a place where the two of them could be alone.

The door opened without notice, and Mallory turned to see Tony come into the room. He swung the door shut, pushed the bolt into place, then turned to her. The sunlight streaming in the windows caught him in clear lights, and she felt her heart catch as he slowly, deliberately let his gaze roam over her. When his eyes lingered at her breasts, she felt an instant, stunning response growing in her.

"My wife," he whispered. "That's incredible."

She went to him, walking into his open arms, and as she held him, she murmured, "Life's incredible."

His hands caressed her back, their heat sending sensations through her that centered in her soul. "It certainly is. It's a miracle," he breathed. Then he stood back and took her by the hand. He led her to the bed, and as they stood facing each other, he gently undid the sapphire pendant that rested between her breasts and laid it on the nightstand.

Then he eased the straps of her silky slip off her shoulders and let the fine material slip to the floor around her ankles. Without a word he took off the white shirt and dark slacks he'd worn for the ceremony, then eased Mallory back onto the bed. "But we don't have time," she whispered. But her tone of voice wasn't exactly filled with conviction.

Tony shifted until he was lying beside her, skin against skin, their heat mingling, and when his hand touched her breasts, she gasped at the pleasures that came without warning. "Time?" Tony whispered. "We've got time." His fingers teased her nipples into hard buds, and an ache was growing in her. "We don't have to go into the city for the flight out for five hours, and I don't know about you, but I don't intend to sit down to a celebration tea with Saxon and Henry."

"But Saxon said..." Her voice trailed off as all of her concentration became focused on the path Tony's hand was taking, over her stomach and downward.

"Saxon and Henry won't miss us for a while, and if they do—" he smiled down at her as she trembled under his caress and arched to his touch "—so what? Saxon let me know he wouldn't mind grandchildren."

"Grandchildren?" she asked in an unsteady voice.

"Yes, you know those little people that we get the fun of creating and the grandparent gets the fun of spoiling."

Children. Tony's child. The thought settled into her heart. Yes, that was right, very right. When his hand found her center, she gasped and her breathing became quick and shallow.

"Let's do a trial run," Tony whispered as she arched toward his touch. "Saxon can wait."

"Yes," Mallory said. Then he had her by her waist, and in one easy movement, she was over him. He gently eased her down until he filled her, and for an eternity they lay there, not moving, just letting the feelings and sensations surround them.

Children, a father and Tony. Mallory trembled from the rocketing sensations that began to build. Yes, she was here, with him, her husband. With her family. "Saxon can wait," she gasped, arching her back.

Henry Welting looked at Saxon sitting with him on the terrace, the fresh and gentle heat of the day bouncing off the worn stones. The new construction had been stilled. Saxon wasn't sure about completing it now. He had a lot of other things to concentrate on, not just surviving because the construction was never ending.

"I think Tony and Mallory might be a bit late," Saxon murmured as he fingered the handle of the teacup resting on the wrought-iron table in front of him.

"Oh, that's—"

"Life," Saxon murmured. "That's life and love."

Henry watched the man smile, and he thought he could see something in his expression that could almost be called peace. Saxon Mills was still Saxon Mills, but there was something about him that was new and, in Henry's opinion, much better.

Henry ignored his tea and smoothed his hand over the front of his double-breasted suit. He could feel the letter he'd brought with him this morning sitting in the inside pocket, the last installment on the investigation of Mallory King. "Saxon?"

"Yes?" he asked as he looked at Henry.

"The investigation on Mallory's finished."

"Yes, it is." He sighed. "I never figured that it would end this way." He sat forward, his elbows resting on the iron table. "My God, Henry, I have a daughter and a son-in-law. And, if things go the way I think they will, I'll have a grandchild. It makes me believe in immortality, not ghosts. My bloodline going on and on."

"That's important to you?"

Saxon shrugged. "I never knew how much I wanted a family—a real family—until now. Yes, it's important to me. I don't know how many years I have left, but they're going to be good ones. I know it."

Henry looked away from Saxon, then stood, having finally decided something he'd been debating since he'd stepped into the house. "I'll be right back," he said, crossing the terrace.

He went through the house to the library, where he walked to the fireplace. He slipped the letter out of his pocket but didn't open it. He knew the contents by heart. Mallory had been born prematurely, eight weeks early. She had probably been conceived after Kate left this place. There was a one-in-a-thousand chance that Mallory King was really Saxon Mills's child.

Henry looked down at the white envelope, then reached for a match from the holder by the hearth. He struck the match, holding the flame to the corner of the envelope until the paper caught fire.

He dropped the burning envelope into the hearth and watched until it was reduced to ashes. Saxon was Henry Welting's client and his friend. The investigation of Mallory King was over. Henry wasn't a gambler, but he was willing to take that one-in-a-thousand chance that Mallory was really Saxon's child.

He turned his back on the ashes in the grate and headed out to see Saxon and toast the new family.

*   *   *   *   *